Murder One

A Colby Tate Mystery

Allen Kent

For information address AllenPearce Publishers,
16635 Hickory Drive, Neosho, MO 64850

AllenPearce Publishers ©  ©

Library of Congress Cataloging-in-Publication Data
Allen Kent
Murder One
Kent, Allen

AllenPearce
PUBLISHERS

ISBN-13: 978-1-7332173-4-7

DEDICATION

To Holly:
my constant support and inspiration

ACKNOWLEDGMENTS

Grateful thanks to my team of readers: my wife Holly, Diane Andris, and Judy Day. You all made this a much better book.
And special thanks to Uvi Poznansky for her wonderful cover!

1

The moment she turned onto the gravel lane that descended the hill into the river bottoms, Brenda Castoe knew Nettie was dead. The woods have a way of letting you know such things. She could see it in the skeleton of the tree that stood beside Nettie's doublewide. The old red oak had been struggling to hang onto its own life for the last couple of years, ravaged by an attack of bark beetles. The top had died back to bare, black tentacles, every one lined with turkey vultures. Brenda said they were thick as pigeons on a powerline, all hunched forward with ugly red heads craned in the direction of Nettie's broken screen door.

Brenda had stopped her Rav4 right there at the top of the downhill and climbed out. Even that high on the hillside, the air was tainted with the smell of death. Other than the distant murmur of the brook that tumbled from a spring at the back of Nettie's property and splashed in front of her ramshackle home, nothing broke the silence of the little valley. Most any time during daylight, you could hear cardinals whistle and gobblers taunt each other on the edges of the meadow behind the house. But Brenda heard nothing. She said it sounded as quiet as, well, death.

She pulled her cell out of the cup holder between the car seats while she was still high enough on the ridge to get a signal and called my office. No sense calling 911. They would just relay the message to me. Most people in the county know my number as well as they know the emergency code. The local phone company here is still privately owned and they made it simple by giving me the same last four as the desk phone at the office. 1188. Folks around here simply know to call "aces and eights."

My name is Colby Tate. And yes. I'm one of the Huckleberry Ridge Tates. For people who grew up here in the county, then moved away, it surprises them when they come back to visit to see me wearing a sheriff's star and not an orange jumpsuit. Jerry Covell tells me that when they come into his Family Market, they'll say to him or to anyone else standing around, "Did we see that you got a Tate serving as sheriff? This can't be the same county I remember!"

They've got good reason for wondering, but it just shows they lost track of me somewhere along the line. For some reason, unbeknownst to me or anyone else, when my cousins were all raising hell and doing what they could to aggravate the law, I got into books. Read everything. In fact, my only venture into larceny was that I found ways to stow an extra book or two in my backpack when I left the county library. I always returned them, mind you, when I'd had time to digest them. I just slipped the extras into the night deposit rather than drop them at the desk where Edith Ellison could tell with a single glance if you were returning more than you'd taken out. Those books, and a couple of great teachers through the years, kept me in school and got me a scholarship afterward. All but eleven of my classmates either got married straight out of high school, went to work for the modular home manufacturer that employs half of Crayton, or joined the Marines. And I don't mean just went in the military. They joined the Marines. Down our way, there's a difference. In fact, I was back at the high school speaking at a career day a few months back when one of my old classmates walked in wearing his uniform. One of the senior girls was just clueless enough to say, "Hey, Louie. I didn't know you was a soldier!" To which Louie said without the slightest trace of good humor, "I'm not a soldier. I'm a Marine"—like all the other branches were just support organizations. Even I did my tour of duty. But that's another story. And I need to get back to the call from Brenda Castoe.

I was sitting with my heels on the desk in what we affectionately call the Blockhouse—a stone bunker of a building on the west side of the square that had once been the old bank. There was a time when every town with more than a thousand breathing citizens had its own K-12 schoolhouse, its own grocery store, and its own bank. The schools across the county have long since been consolidated, placed out in the middle of a cornfield far enough from everyone that every kid has to be bussed, but no community can lay claim to the school being theirs. That happened long enough ago that the internecine squabbles that once bordered on something akin to gang warfare have simmered down to snide references to rival towns and family origins.

We've managed to keep Jerry's Family Market alive by stubbornly paying the extra five to ten percent it costs to keep one of our neighbors in business. But the bank closed, replaced out on the highway by a branch of one of the city banks. Two tellers, an ATM, and a drive-up window. The city police laid claim early to space in the old junior high/high school cum city hall. So when the sheriff's department decided to relocate from a drafty metal building on North Madison Street, we got the old bank building. In some ways, we were the lucky ones. The vault gives us a secure evidence room, and two of the offices in the back were converted to a jail. I have the little glassed cubicle that once put the loan officer right up front where everyone could see her. But I've let my story get away from me again.

"Sheriff," Brenda Castoe said when she called, "I'm out on the road above Nettie Suskey's place, and things don't look right. I'd just as soon not go down there without someone with me."

I dropped the booted heels to the floor and asked what made her nervous.

"Vultures," she said, and told me about the buzzards, the putrid odor, and the quiet. Any two of the three would have been enough to convince me she had good reason to stay put until help arrived. Vultures can smell death from miles away and, though it's not

3

uncommon for them to roost on bare branches, they generally don't choose to be that close to a house. And Nettie's valley is *never* quiet.

My chief deputy is Grace Torres. On that particular afternoon, Grace was over in the courthouse giving testimony in a case involving the theft of toys from a storage unit where the police department keeps its stock of donations until our local "Christmas for Kids" day rolls around. A little hard to believe, isn't it? That someone would be stupid enough to break into the place the police store toys people have donated to give to poor kids at Christmas? We caught the three numbskulls when they tried to make a deal with another Christmas charity up in Greene County. Said they had a bunch of never-been-opened toys they would sell real cheap. Fortunately for the thieves, they were also from Greene County. If Judge Werner had really wanted to punish them, he would have sentenced them to having to live down here among the citizens of Crayton for the next ten years. People here have absolutely no tolerance for stealing toys from kids. Grace had responded to the call from the Greene County charity, had made the arrest, and was over in the courthouse when Brenda called.

Rocky D'Amico, who we call our Jail Commander, watches over the rare prisoner we might be holding, keeps an eye on the evidence room, and cruises the area just beyond the city limits every few hours. Rocky's in his late fifties, about sixty pounds on the heavy side, and as friendly a guy as Mr. Rogers. People around Crayton love him, but he's slow on the hoof and a heart attack waiting to happen. I try to leave Rocky within spitting distance of the office.

That would leave Frankie Ritter to go out to Nettie's if I didn't. He patrols the north half of the county and would probably be closer. But Frankie has his own set of issues. He's a small, weasel-eyed man with a pencil-thin mustache who keeps an obstacle course in the backyard of his place up in Willston. That's a wide spot in the road about halfway between here and the county line.

The first time I visited his house, I was responding to a call from a neighbor who reported shots fired from the direction of Frankie's back yard. I found him practicing a "drop, draw, and roll" maneuver under a two-foot high bar, drawing his weapon as he tumbled and swinging back up onto one knee to fire off a shot at a silhouette target he'd braced against a pile of sandbags. The closest I've come to letting one of the deputies go is when Frankie tested the move when responding to a backup call from a state trooper.

The patrolman had chased down and nosed in front of a speeding vehicle with deeply tinted windows, but couldn't get anyone to leave the car. Frankie pulled up nose-to-nose with the trooper's vehicle on the shoulder of the two-lane road, threw open the door of his own squad car, and practiced his "roll and draw" into a marshy roadside ditch. In the heat of battle, he'd left the car running, failed to shift into park, and his empty cruiser rammed the trooper's front fender. Frankie heard the collision, thought the suspect had surged his own vehicle forward into the patrolman's, and said he would have fired if he hadn't been screened from his target by a thick stand of cattails. This may sound like a pretty questionable bunch to be providing law enforcement to a county of just under 50,000, but we get the job done and people generally feel safe and watched after.

The other two deputies are night patrol, so when Brenda called, I really had no choice but to head out there myself. It's about a twenty-five-minute drive on winding, two-lane roads overhung by oak and hickory. I told Brenda to just sit tight and wait till I got there.

I can't say that I know Brenda Castoe that well. She lives up in Springfield and works for one of those medical alert companies. Some job that takes her around to check up on all the people who subscribe to their service. So we run into each other every now and again. A pleasant woman. Maybe forty-five and what I hear referred to as "full-figured." She's always dresses in Sunday-go-to-church clothes, even when she's visiting someone way out in the hills. Maybe that's something the job requires, but I suspect it has more to do with her religion. Mid-calf dresses and long hair rolled up on her head. The dresses have a way of making me feel underdressed when I'm around her, like a sheriff shouldn't be wearing jeans, even if they're pretty new and worn with a neatly-pressed khaki uniform shirt.

She was waiting in her Toyota, but climbed out when I turned down off the ridge and pulled up beside her. As I expected, she was wearing a pretty dress in a rose color, but had on shoes my mother would have labeled "sensible." Good solid soles and heels.

"Sorry to drag you out here, Sheriff," she said, which showed we really didn't know each other all that well. Everyone in the county calls me Tate. "But things just don't look right to me. I called down the hill after I phoned, and nobody came to the door. And that flock of buzzards didn't budge."

I wanted to tell her that a flock of vultures is called a committee, one of those bits of trivia I picked up from all that reading. But I've found that correcting people on things that don't matter much isn't a good way to connect. It also makes you look like a know-it-all—something some folks here already think anyway. I work hard at not adding to the perception.

I could smell death on the air from where we were and listened for a moment to the quiet of the valley below. "Yeah," I told Brenda, "I think you made a good decision. Things don't seem right. You out here for one of your visits?" It seemed like a pretty obvious thing to be asking. But when something doesn't look right, I always like to know what brought people to that place at that time.

"Yes. I try to drop by at least once a month. Test the alert systems and make sure our clients are happy. I was over at the Gilreaths' and thought I'd swing by while I was this close."

"And how is Maribel?" Maribel Gilreath is a little like Nettie, but a widow. Nettie has just chosen to stay single. Both live by themselves, don't have any living kin to speak of, and are too old to be out here in the woods alone. But God help the concerned soul who tries to tell them that.

Brenda's smile was a little sad. "Same old Maribel. She still drives that old pickup into town for groceries but has to use a walker to get around the house. I asked her how she gets her foot from the gas to the brake. She told me she drives in low all the time, and there's only one stop sign between her place and the market. If there's no traffic coming, she doesn't stop. That way she only has to move the leg once as she gets close to the store, and she has plenty of time to plan for it."

I couldn't help but chuckle. "Yup. That's Maribel. I stopped her once for going so slow. It was when I first came back and didn't know her truck. Thought I was tailing a drunk. She has blocks taped to the pedals so she can reach them."

"You couldn't get her off the road?"

"She hadn't done anything wrong. Had a valid license. The county license people don't seem to have the heart to turn some of those old-timers down."

Brenda sniffed. "I hope she decides to give it up before she meets someone at that stop sign and doesn't have time to get that leg in motion."

"We can hope," I said. "Let's go check on Nettie."

We left Brenda's car where she'd parked it and rolled slowly down the hill toward the trailer in my Explorer. The buzzards wagged their hideous heads from house to car and back. A couple spread their wings like sails and tried to look threatening. None left the dying oak. I parked by the walk to Nettie's sagging steps and we both sat for a moment, looking at the silent house. As soon as I opened my door, we knew Brenda's fears were founded. Death hung in the air like swamp gas.

"Oh, dear Lord," she murmured, covering her nose and mouth with a quivering hand. I reached over and flipped open the glovebox, pulling out a thick fiber mask.

"You'd better wait here." I fixed it over my face and pulled the elastic straps back over my head.

Brenda shook her head. "I'd like to come in. I've been a hospice nurse. This won't be anything I haven't seen before. And she's my client." She fished a handkerchief from her knock-off Louis Vuitton handbag.

I didn't argue. There are plenty of things I prefer to do completely on my own, but finding a dead body isn't one of them. We both slid from the Explorer and Brenda followed me up onto the porch.

The screen door was latched but not locked. The inside wooden door was ajar and the stink of decomposition poured out like raw sewage from a ruptured septic tank. I pushed it open and noticed then what I should have seen when I drove up. Every curtain was closed tight. The inside was pitch dark. Beneath the suffocating scent of death, I picked up a more permanent stale mustiness.

"Anybody home?" I yelled, knowing there would be no answer. We both eased into the dusky living room and stood for a moment, letting our eyes adjust. And there she was, sitting upright in a faded green overstuffed chair with her head lolled back, eyes bulging, and mouth agape. Her face and hands were as blue-white as her wild shock of unkempt hair. Eyes I remembered as pale blue had faded to dull gray. I pulled a pair of clean cotton gloves from my pocket, something I've learned to carry for just these occasions, and stepped to the wall. Using just a fingernail, I flipped on the light. The dark had been kind to Nettie. In the light, we could see the work of rodents that shared the house. A rat the size of a red squirrel skittered from beneath her chair and disappeared under a sofa that filled most of one wall.

"Oh, my God!" Brenda wheezed. She had pulled the neck of that rose dress up across her face.

"Not exactly hospice," I guessed, stepping closer to the corpse where I could have a better look. Brenda didn't say anything and hung back by the door.

"Been dead a few days," I said, mainly to myself. "You must be the first person to come by." Brenda grunted an acknowledgement.

Though Nettie had practically nothing in the house, her few belongings were scattered recklessly about the room. A corner china cabinet stood open, most of its porcelain contents shattered into delicately painted shards that covered the floor like a spilled basket of flower petals.

I crouched near the arm of the chair. "That face looks like sheer terror. Like she was frightened to death."

Brenda took a step closer. "You're too new to this job, Sheriff. A heart attack or suffocation will do that to a person. Crushing pain or the inability to draw a breath. Pretty terrifying. I wonder why she didn't trigger her alert?" The small white pendant with its red button hung uselessly about the woman's neck.

I pointed at dark bruises across the center of both forearms. "Depending on what happened, she may not have had time. Looks like she was pinned down." I pulled out my pocket knife, an eight-inch Buck knife I'd guess every able-bodied male in the county over the age of six carries somewhere on his person. Next to a cell phone, it's about the most useful tool one can have. I flipped open the blade, slipped the back into the cup of Nettie's partially clawed right hand, and lifted it off the arm of the chair.

"Like I thought," I told Brenda. "Rigor has started to relax. She's been dead a couple of days. And look here." I pointed with my free hand at traces of blood on the tips of the woman's fingernails. "She struggled with someone." I gently returned the hand to its resting place and tucked the knife back in my pocket. "Time to call in the state police."

Brenda retreated toward the door. "Why would anyone want to murder old Nettie?" she murmured. "The woman has nothing and wouldn't harm a fly."

I ushered Brenda back onto the porch and pulled the door partially shut behind me. "Nothing but what you see around you. If what I hear is right, she owns about 300 acres of timberland behind here along the creek."

9

Brenda lowered the neck of her dress and smoothed it back into place, glancing about. "But isn't this all part of what's supposed to be flooded by the water project? Become part of the new reservoir?"

"Yup. Part of the eminent domain land. Nettie's been raising hell about it. But she hasn't been able to slow anything down. I can't see any reason someone would want her out of the way when her complaining hasn't had any effect." I pulled open the passenger side of the patrol car and waved Brenda in. "We need to get back up on the ridge road where I can call Springfield."

"She's been pretty upset," the woman murmured as she slid into the seat. "But who would want to kill Nettie Suskey?"

2

A guy as new to the job as I am wants to sound calm and confident when making a pronouncement at a crime scene in front of someone who's likely to talk about it. At the same time, it made me nervous as hell to think someone had murdered a harmless old woman in my county. Though I'd been on the job less than a year, I'd already had two occasions to use my gloves on a body: a girl not even out of high school who didn't feel like she needed to heed the "don't text and drive" warnings, and a guy I'd gone to school with who, to no one's surprise, blew himself up overcooking a batch of meth. But Nettie was one of those "I don't think she has an enemy in the world" kind of people who bothered no one. She drove her old open-sided jeep into the Methodist church every Sunday and again on Wednesday nights for the women's group, and didn't seem to have enough in her old trailer to attract anyone's attention. It was a shot of adrenalin to finally have a legitimate murder case, but I wasn't at all thrilled by what it said about the spot I'd decided was the right place to settle down .

After taking Brenda back up to her car, I'd called the coroner and state police and waited until both arrived. Our local coroner is Chase Backman who runs the funeral home, assisted living center, and ambulance service: what the locals jokingly call "full-service dying." But Chase is an honest man, and people are happy to trust their declining years to his care. Plus, I haven't seen others clambering to take business from him. Chase knows when a job requires more than his forensic skills, which are limited mainly to taking a rough stab at time of death. When he and the state trooper arrived, we photographed the body from every angle, and he had

Nettie taken right up to the morgue in Springfield.

The patrolman who showed up within minutes of Chase was Dave Johansson, another guy as honest as the day is long, but not an investigator.

"You look around much more inside?" he asked after we'd finished with the body.

"No. Just enough to know someone killed Nettie and ransacked the place. I didn't want to do any more poking about until I had a little more forensic experience with me."

He glanced about the living room. "Unfortunately, that wouldn't be me. But someone was either looking for something to steal or wanted us to think so. You didn't look in the other rooms?"

"Waiting for you." I led him down a short hall to the right into a bedroom. There wasn't much to check in there either, but all of it was scattered about like a twister had been through the room. The double-bed mattress was thrown off its metal frame, the clothes from the single dresser strewn haphazardly across the floor. An upholstered, roll-armed chair was upside down, its cross-braced springs visible and the cushion thrown against one wall. Clothes in a small closet with a bi-fold door still hung on the rod, but pushed to one side. The few boxes from a narrow shelf above were upended beneath them.

"For being out here where no one could hear and it's unlikely anyone would come by, this search looks kind of frantic," Johansson said. He did a quick walk-through of the rest of the trailer with me, suggested we secure the place until he could get a specialist on the scene, and called in the request to his regional headquarters. I found Grace back in the office when I called, asked her to bring out a Canadian bacon and pineapple pizza from the Woodshed with a thermos of coffee, and told her I'd be camping out overnight. She had the "on-call." Then I planted the squad car at the end of the path to Nettie's steps and waited for dinner.

I've told you what you need to know to understand why Rocky and Frankie weren't chosen as Chief Deputy. And our two night guys work nights because they want to. Larry Newby's a retired security guy from Jack Henry and Associates and is about as reliable as an old Swiss clock. But he likes to be home during the day. He finishes his shift at 4:00 a.m., sleeps until just after noon, then works in his garden or woodshop until he comes on duty at 8:00. If I tried to change his hours, he'd be gone in a heartbeat.

Bobby Lule roams the county between midnight and when we open the office at 8:00. He's the other Latino on the force, one of those ex-marines I was telling you about. A solitary guy whose personal version of PTSD inclines him to want to be alone. But when trouble raises its ugly head early in the morning, Bobby's not shy about taking it on and calling for help when he needs it. The county's in good hands at night.

But that pretty well left Grace as my choice for Chief Deputy—that, or I hired someone new. Just after I got elected, I stopped in on Jerry at Family Market who probably has a better sense for what's happening around the county than anyone in town. He's usually behind the meat counter slicing and wrapping the porkchops that bring people in from as far west as the Oklahoma line. He'll throw out a bright "Good morning! And what's new in your world?" and keeps working while people tell him everything that's been on their minds. He's sort of like our father-confessor, hairdresser, and best buddy all rolled into one. And he keeps things pretty much to himself, so no one's ever able to come back at him with an "I didn't expect you to be spreading that about." For some reason, Jerry decided to take the new sheriff under his well-informed wing and started by recommending Grace.

"You won't find a better Deputy Sheriff," he told me while slicing a couple of pounds of sharp cheddar for a brats-and-burgers open house we were planning to welcome me into office. "The Torres family's well-respected by everyone. Grace speaks both Spanish and English as first languages, and she's smart as a whip. Nothing escapes that girl."

"Almost too pretty," I suggested.

Jerry looked up from his cheese slicer with a sharp enough glare to remind me what a dumb thing that was to say. He didn't stop with just the look. "Better keep that comment to yourself. We don't get quite as PC around here as lots of places. But if Grace got wind that she'd been passed over because you thought her too pretty for the job, you'd never hear the end of it. Until next election. Then you'd be gone."

"I was just meaning that I worry people might not take her as seriously as they need to," I fumbled. "Some smartass who thinks he's being pulled over by Jennifer Lopez and wants to impress her with what a macho sonofabitch he is."

Jerry chuckled. "It would only happen once. I guarantee you, this isn't the kind of grace Reverend Latimer's doling out. You haven't been back in town long enough to have seen our Grace in action."

I had my chance two days later. Cille Hubbard, who'd been living by herself on a three-acre spread about a mile east of town, had been moved into assisted living by her kids. The next week, true to a grapevine that sweeps our county in a way that would make Facebook green with envy, someone broke into the empty house and ransacked it, taking everything Cille's daughters hadn't moved with her. One of the girls stopped by to mow the lawn and make sure the power had been turned off and called in the robbery. It was my first visit to a scene with Grace Torres.

"Don't mow the lawn," Grace told the daughter as we completed our walk-through. She answered the woman's surprised look with, "They left that big flat-screen on the wall in the living room and the riding mower that's chained to the tree out back. That means they didn't have bolt cutters and enough room in whatever they were driving to take the TV. I'm guessing they'll watch the place for a day to see if the break-in's been discovered. When they think it hasn't, they'll be back with a pickup and something to cut that mower loose."

The daughter looked dubiously at the heavy zero-turn mower.

"There was no key here for it. It would be hard to lift into a truck."

Grace sniffed, glancing down at the key the woman now held. "Look at how basic that thing is. And there are about a dozen stock keys for those mowers. If this is the bunch that's been hitting places like this around the county, they have what they need to start it or can hotwire the thing. Don't mow the lawn. I'll hang out here the next couple of nights."

Just after 1:00 a.m. that night, the radio beside my bed blared, "Bobby or Larry? One of you close to the Hubbard place? I've got company and could use some backup."

I was there fifteen minutes later, pulling into the Hubbard drive right in front of Larry Newby. We both bailed from our cruisers behind sheltering doors, weapons drawn.

"Got things under control," Grace called from the house. "Come on in."

The pair that were sprawled face-down on the living room carpet, wrists cuffed, were classic meth heads: bone-thin as worm-ravaged mongrels, rheumy-eyed with pupils the size of dimes, and teeth that looked like they'd been through a brush fire. I couldn't tell if their squirming and twitching was drug-induced or because one's nose had been flattened across his face like a piece of roadkill. The other was trying to keep weight off a dislocated shoulder. A crimson stain continued to spread beneath the smashed face. The man with the shoulder was more concerned about other injuries.

"She smashed my nuts," he gurgled through a mouthful of snot. "I know one of 'em's ruptured. I'm gonna sue the shit out of all of you."

Grace nodded toward an eight-inch blade a few inches from the man's hip. "Better get a photo of that. It'll have his prints all over it. He was dumb enough to pull it when I confronted the sonofabitch."

Officer Newby was wrestling the perp with the smashed face to his feet. "And what happened to this piece of work?"

"Look underneath him there. He was out back cutting the mower loose. He was stupid enough to pull that thing and charge through from the kitchen when he heard his buddy here go down." A rubber-gripped, .38 caliber Smith and Wesson lay beneath him on the caramel shag, a few inches from the widening red stain. Grace held up her arm to display the blood-splattered elbow of her uniform shirt. "Ran into this," she said.

No one complained when Grace was named Deputy Sheriff. To some folks around town, she's simply known as Amazing Grace. To me, she's proven a dozen times since that she was the right pretty face for the job.

I'd backed the Explorer out of sight behind a birch clump and was kicked back, listening to a Grisham audiobook on my phone when I heard her coming down the hill with the pizza. She seemed to know where I'd be hiding and turned in beside me, her driver's window a few feet from mine.

"Medium Canadian bacon and pineapple—and I assumed you'd want a large diet Coke with that. Right?" The pizza box slid through the window, followed by a 44-ounce styrofoam cup and a fistful of napkins.

I chuckled at the size of the drink. "*This* should help keep me awake. Have you had dinner? I can probably manage about two-thirds of this pizza, so you may as well help me with the other third."

Grace held up her own 32-ounce drink. "I was hoping you might ask and had them put jalapenos on half of it. You can pick them off if you decide you want two-thirds. Hang on. I'll pull the car out of the way." A moment later, she slid into the passenger seat and reached back for a slice of the pie I'd deposited behind me.

Though I'd given permission and chose to myself, Grace refused to wear jeans with her uniform shirt. Part of it, I guessed was that she knew it helped her look "official" if she had on the full uniform. But it was also because she looked so damn good in the official pants. Leaning over the seat stretched the whole outfit even tighter over a frame that already displayed it like a photo shoot. I told myself every day that there was something fundamentally unprofessional about feeling your insides stir every time your chief deputy reached for a binder on a top shelf. But they did, and there wasn't a whole lot I could do about it.

"Marti gave me the basics when I got back from court," she said, cupping the pizza slice to keep the peppers and pineapple off her lap. "I knew you'd have your hands full, so didn't call. But what have you been thinking?"

I'd found one of her jalapenos on my wedge and was desperately slurping coke in an effort to keep from looking like I couldn't handle my peppers. I let the fizz bubble away some of the burn, checked over the rest of my slice for any other green flecks, and set my cup in the holder between the seats.

"The place is a mess. All torn up to look like a robbery. But you know as well as I do that Nettie didn't have anything. I can't see anyone killing her just to steal from an old, dirt-poor woman."

Grace nodded, chewing on a pepper-riddled slice with a relish I knew was mainly for my benefit. "The timing can't be coincidental. The settlements are starting to be negotiated for the land in the flood zone. Had Nettie been given an offer?"

"They haven't gone out yet, as far as I know. And Jerry keeps pretty close track of this kind of thing. The assessments were finished two months ago, but we'd have heard if someone had been made an offer."

"Pretty valuable land."

"Yeah. Maybe the best tract in the flood zone."

"Who stands to benefit if Nettie's out of the way?"

I took a bite of the side of my slice I knew had been farthest from the peppers.

"I got a feeling," I said, looking past Grace in the waning light at the shadowy shell of the trailer, "that figuring that out is going to be one helluva lot harder than either of us can imagine."

3

The sound of tires struggling to grip the steep downhill into the valley pulled me from a dream in which I was arguing with an Iraqi tribal leader about why we needed to conduct a house-to-house search of his village. I was losing and welcomed being dragged back into consciousness by the unmarked Chevy Tahoe. I stretched upright, slapped my cheeks a few times to give them a little color, and swung out of the car like I'd been staring intently at Nettie's screen door all night. The SUV pulled up opposite me, pointed the other way with the driver hidden. The investigator that stepped out couldn't have looked less like State Trooper Dave Johansson. She wasn't much taller than the top of the Tahoe, with short brown hair, dark almond eyes, and an oval face that I'd rate on the pretty side of cute. She grinned across at me like she knew I was sizing her up.

"So the chief drew the night watch," she said, staying where she was and letting me do the walking.

"I was out here. And my deputy was in court all day. She needed a good night's sleep."

"She was in early. I called on my way down to see where I should meet you."

"Yeah. She's a bit compulsive that way. But she must have given you good directions. This isn't an easy place to find. Nettie used a post office box and had no address for your GPS." I rounded the end of the Explorer and had a look at the rest of the state investigator. Trim jeans. A light blue, long-sleeved shirt under a tan jacket with the state patrol emblem on the pocket. I'm six-three with shoes on, and she came about to my shoulder. I extended a hand.

"Colby Tate. Most people call me Tate."

Her grasp was surprisingly firm and confident. "I gathered that from your deputy. I'm officer Joseph. Mara Joseph. I've been asked to help with your investigation. You can call me whatever you like."

"Mara," I said, swept back a lifetime to a small church not more than ten miles from where we stood. "The name taken by Naomi when she returned to Bethlehem."

"Well, well! A sheriff who knows his Tanakh."

I smiled enough to let her know it was a friendly correction and said, "Old Testament to the people down here. You don't grow up in these hills without being schooled in the scripture. But Tanakh and Mara Joseph? I'd guess you were schooled in Torah and Talmud."

Mara Joseph cocked her head to one side. "I don't think I've ever had a first conversation when I arrived at a crime scene that was quite like this. But, yes. You're right. My family's Jewish."

My smile tightened into an embarrassed grin. "Sorry, Officer Joseph. You'll have to excuse me. I've always been something of a language nut, and I couldn't help myself. Mara's a pretty name. As I recall, it means 'bitter' in Hebrew."

Her head stayed slightly cocked and her brow furrowed over those captivating dark eyes. "I heard you were a Marine interpreter in Iraq. Then did a stint with the State Department in the same kind of role somewhere in the Middle East. Not what I would have expected of a rural sheriff in this part of the state. Did your interpreting include Hebrew?"

"I'm really not at all fluent in Hebrew. Better Arabic and Farsi. But I remembered Mara from my Bible study as a kid."

She raised an amused brow. "Mara also means 'comes from the sea.' Some days I fit one definition. Some days, the other. When I'm on a murder investigation, I lean toward bitter."

"Well, Tate's a Norse name that means 'cheerful.' So if we're going to work this together, on your bitter days, maybe I can carry us."

Her smile relaxed. "Okay, Tate. And while we're in the 'learning each other's names' stage, what does Colby mean?"

I shrugged loosely, liking this woman just for being willing to play along with my awkward weirdness. "Also Norse. It means 'a settlement of swarthy people.' I don't think that will help us much."

She laughed lightly. "*Swarthy*? Not a word I hear in everyday conversation."

"It's more descriptive than 'dark-skinned.' And those are loaded words nowadays."

The laugh deepened. "This is going to be an interesting assignment, Tate. I've already learned more than in any other ten minutes this month."

"I'll try to control myself. But do I hear a little St. Louis in your voice?"

She again arched a brow. "Pretty well-trained ear! University City. My family's part of the old Jewish community there."

"Welcome to the buckle of the Bible Belt," I said. "But you have one thing working in your favor. No one else down here knows Mara Joseph sounds Jewish."

She shrugged lightly. "I'm not concerned. Now, to get to a little business." She handed me a brief report. "Death by suffocation. The victim appears to have attempted to fight off her assailant and had traces of blood and skin beneath the fingernails of her right hand. Bruising on the wrists indicate she was being tightly held by an assailant who pinned her in the chair in which she was found and forced an object over her mouth and nose." Pretty much the way I'd read it when I checked the body.

Mara Joseph was a one-person forensics team. While I dusted for prints, she systematically worked her way through Nettie's house and scattered belongings: photographing, picking up and cataloging samples, taking notes, and sketching diagrams. For a dilapidated doublewide in the woods, the trailer looked like it had been surprisingly neat before the perp tore it apart. Spare on furnishings and clothing, with only a dozen pots and pans, and absent the kind of knickknacks you expect to find lining shelves and stuffing glass-fronted cabinets in a single old lady's living space. She had an apartment-sized washer and dryer, almost new, and a four-burner stove connected to a propane tank behind the house. The ancient oak bed, dresser, and rocking chair summed up the furnishings in the bedroom. The other spare room had been converted into what you might call a study: a straight-backed chair of the same native wood, open-faced desk, and two-drawer gray metal filing cabinet, all dumped onto the floor. What looked like a handmade bookshelf of white oak had held three narrow shelves of books: a worn Bible and a collection of works by early American writers that looked like she'd bought them as a set maybe thirty or forty years ago: Hawthorne, Cooper, Longfellow, Twain, and a dozen more that now littered a room-sized area rug. Joseph spent the better part of two hours examining every scrap of paper and thumbing through every book.

"Any idea how this woman made a living?" she asked after re-shelving a final volume that contained Jack London's *White Fang* and *Call of the Wild*.

I sent the last fingerprint I'd lifted and photographed to the crime lab via my cellphone and squatted on my haunches to stretch cramps from my back and thighs. "Recently? I really have no idea. When I lived here before, she worked part-time in the cafeteria in the elementary school. All the kids called her Aunt Nettie. Why do you ask?"

Mara waved a hand over the papers she'd placed on the desk and filing cabinet. "I've gone through every file and piece of mail in this house and there's nothing related to money. No bank records. No Social Security reports. Not even Medicare or Medicaid information. I'd think an old single woman living out here would be getting some kind of benefits."

That made sense to me. I'd read recently that government transfer payments were the single largest source of income in the county, which struck me as ironic at the time since everyone I know here is so anxious to keep government out of their lives. I glanced about the room. "Maybe that's what the search was for. Someone wanted those records. Or there's a file somewhere we haven't come across."

"If there is, it's not in the trailer," Mara said emphatically. "Maybe in that little shed out back."

I scribbled a list of notes in my pocket pad. *Check with Doc Waterman about how Nettie paid her bills. See what Jerry knows at Family Market. Stop by the branch bank to check on accounts. Find out where Nettie purchased her washer and dryer and how she paid.* It was then my phone buzzed with the expanded pathology report. I read it while Mara added to her own notes.

"Yup. She was suffocated but not strangled," I said. "She'd been dead about forty-eight hours. It looks like both arms were restrained. Whoever killed Nettie should have scratches on skin that would have been exposed during the struggle. They're typing and running a DNA profile on the tissue."

Mara gave a quiet *humph* under her breath. "We can't assume the scratches will have been on exposed skin. She might have forced a hand up under a shirt or blouse or scratched at a shin. Hard to guess. But a DNA sample might be all we need. There's no sign of forced entry, and it's very likely this was someone she knew. We just need to start watching for scratches and getting cheek swabs of everyone who might be a possibility."

"I wouldn't put much weight on the forced-entry. No one here locks their doors."

"Even out here in the woods?" she asked as she led me out to take a look in the shed.

"Especially out here. Who's going to bother an old trailer this far off the road?"

"Yeah. Right," Joseph said cynically. "That's why we're here investigating her murder."

"You're right. Dumb thing to say," I conceded. "But there's a general philosophy around that if someone's going to break in, they'll break in. If the door's unlocked, at least your door and windows won't get damaged."

"Makes perfect sense," Joseph snickered.

The shed was one of those pre-fabs, built on skids and sold in parking lots at feed and hardware stores. Nettie used it as a tool shed. It was as neat and spare as I'd imagined the inside of her trailer to have been. Rakes, hoes, and shovels hung on hooks along one wall. Two weed-eaters on the other. A small tiller and gas push mower filled most of the floor. Two five-gallon gas cans stood in a corner, one with "50:1" written on the side with a black marker. A shelf across the back held a Poulan chain saw with a sixteen-inch bar and a gallon of chain bar oil.

Joseph stepped in between the mower and tiller. "No place in here that she might have had something hidden. If they checked in here, they didn't even have to move anything. What's this 50:1?"

I couldn't suppress a chuckle. "They didn't teach you that at U. City High School? That's a gas-oil mix for the weed-eaters and chain saw."

She grinned over at me. "I'm sure our gardener would have known."

I didn't grin back. Maybe the Jewish part wouldn't bother people down here, but a comment like that would. "When we're visiting with the folks around," I cautioned, "that's the kind of remark I'd keep to myself."

Joseph's cheeks flushed. "Yes. You're right. *My* dumb thing to say. I'll be more careful."

We exited the shed, did a thorough walk-about of the small yard and garden area without seeing anything helpful, and went back to the cars.

"The closest neighbor's a local artist who works out of a cabin up on the other side of the valley," I told her. "In the winter, I think he can probably see Nettie's place from his and can hear everything that goes on down here. Too grown-over now, but he may have heard cars coming down the hill. Let's grab some lunch, talk over what we have in our notes, and we can go see Darnell. He's worth a visit, even if he doesn't know anything."

4

What Darnell Budgeon called a cabin was more a long, cedar log studio with a small kitchen and bedroom cobbled onto one end. The kitchen looked out onto the studio over a waist-high bar made of a couple of two-foot wide sycamore slabs, joined along one edge so the halves mirrored each other. Darnell used the kitchen side of the bar as his eating table and the studio side to mix paint, clean brushes, and stack assorted pieces of equipment he used to stretch canvases and make frames. The place smelled of raw umber, burnt sienna, and turpentine. He came to the door wiping both hands and a sable brush on an apron that looked like a Jackson Pollack and would probably stand on its own if he hadn't had it strapped about his neck.

Darnell's a wiry bit of a man with a body full of nervous tics that cause head, feet, and every member in between to be in constant motion unless he's standing in front of an easel. Then he's still as a setter holding point on a covey of quail.

"Well, I'll swan, Tate!" he said, talking to me but bobbing and nodding appreciatively in front of Joseph. "Haven't seen you in a coon's age. What brings you and this . . ." His eyes locked on the patch on Joseph's jacket, ". . . this fine representative of the law out here this morning?" He danced aside and let me usher Joseph into the studio.

"This is Inspector Mara Joseph of the State Police," I said as she tried to chase one of Darnell's weaving hands long enough to shake it. He nodded and grinned over at me as if to say, "You did all right to find this one, Tate. I approve."

I jumped in quickly enough to keep him from turning his thoughts into words. "I hate to trouble you, Darnell, but there's been some trouble down in the valley."

"You mean them Greaves working their way into Nettie's timber? I wondered if she'd be calling you in on that." I saw Joseph's eyes sweep the room, stop and widen when they fell on a six-by-ten-foot painting of a Civil War hospital scene. I decided to get business out of the way before introducing her to the unlikely prodigy that was Darnell Budgeon, so asked, "What have the Greaves been up to?"

Darnell twitched his way back to the open doorway, waving the brush in his hand down in the direction of Nettie's trailer that was somewhere off to the right behind a screen of cedar and hardwoods.

"They been logging the back part of their stand, trying to get what they can cut and sold before the valley's flooded. I can tell from the sound of their saws where they're working. This last few weeks, they've been crossed over onto Nettie's land."

Joseph had joined us at the door. "Maybe they had her permission," she suggested.

Darnell twitched a headshake. "No way. You know them Greaves, Tate. Now, I'm a guy who can say I never met a man I couldn't see some good in. Even the worst kind's got some little shred of decency, somewhere down deep. Except them Greaves. Not a single spit of human kindness between the two of them. That right, Tate? They even hates each other."

"Not the most likable folks," I agreed.

Darnell snorted. "I'd guess the *least* likable. Name one other person in the county who comes close to being as cussed mean and ornery as either one of them Greaves. Was you back in town when the one shot the other? Shot him in the back, right in the wing bone, cause they was fighting over who had to kill a chicken for dinner. Only worthwhile thing they ever did for this county was to set a bad example. Nettie can't abide either one of them. She'd never let them take some of her trees."

Joseph stepped out onto the porch and peered down into the

valley. "Is this serious business? Cutting timber off someone else's land?"

"Not quite up there with rustling someone's cattle," I told her. "But only a notch below. If you can prove it to a judge, he'll award three times the estimated value of the trees taken."

"And how much value do they have?"

"Right now? Some good straight walnut are bringing upwards of a thousand dollars if they've got size. And white oak is doing about as well this year."

Joseph puffed a "*whew*" through pursed lips. "Maybe Nettie confronted them and threatened to turn them in."

"A good place to start," I agreed. "And you may as well meet the two human beings that don't have a spit of goodness between the two of them."

Darnell jerked even more nervously beside me. "She said 'Maybe Nettie confronted them.' Has something happened to Nettie, Tate?"

I kept my eyes on the trees across the road. "I'm afraid so, Darnell. We found her dead yesterday morning in her trailer. Looks like she was smothered."

A stuttered groan welled up in Darnell's chest. "Oh, Tate. Who would do such a thing? I didn't ever see much of the old lady, but she was good people."

I laid a hand on his shivering shoulder. "Yes, she was, Darnell. Have you seen or heard anything else that might be helpful?"

He seemed to calm for a moment as he thought. "In the last few days? Nothing, Tate. I haven't even heard the Greaves cutting. It's been quiet."

I glanced over at Joseph. "We'd better go see why the Greaves decided to stop taking trees. But before we head out, I saw you looking at the painting Darnell's working on." We turned back into the cabin.

"It's masterful," Joseph murmured, walking over to bend close to the canvas. "I don't believe I've ever seen anything quite like it."

Darnell danced over beside her and immediately calmed as he stood in front of the canvas. "Isn't nothing like it. Just finishing it up for the old Ray House up at Wilson's Creek."

"The National Battlefield?"

Darnell forced an exaggerated nod. "The old house was the field hospital for the Confederates."

Joseph looked the painting over more carefully and pointed at a blood-stained body stretched on a central table. "This must be General Lyon."

Darnell's face spread into an appreciative grin. "You know your Civil War history."

"I wish," Joseph said with a chuckle. "I had family down from St. Louis two weekends ago and we toured the battlefield."

"You got a good memory then. Yep. That's General Lyon. This should be hanging up there next time you visit."

"It's amazing," Joseph said. "Another reason to take people over there, now that I've met the artist."

Darnell beamed. "You've helped me finish it up. I've been worrying over this one nurse's face." He pointed with his brush at a partially completed figure beside the wounded general. "I wanted this nurse to be someone kind of strong, but angel-like. Then she walks through my door this morning."

Rather than blushing, Joseph's face seemed to darken, her mouth tightening. "People tell me I could use a little more compassion. So you'll have to improvise."

Darnell's smile softened. "I'm an artist. And I see what I see."

Back in the Explorer, Joseph sat silently while I drove along the ridge toward the Greaves place.

"Quite a talent," she said finally. "How does he paint like that with whatever his disorder is?"

"You saw how he settled down when he was with you by the painting. He's that way when he's working. Hand's as steady as a watchmaker. Amazing thing to see."

"I hope he wasn't serious about painting me in."

"I think he was. Darnell isn't much of one to joke around." I glanced over as I turned off the ridge and slowed to a crawl, carefully guiding the cruiser down the rutted dirt track that descended into what locals call Blackjack Holler. A hand-painted sign nailed to a thick hickory warned "No Trespassers—and that means YOU."

"And I'd have to agree with him. He's got a good eye for what will look right in his paintings."

Joseph sniffed. "Most of the people who know me would hardly say I'm the picture of the angel of mercy."

"Sounds like he's been looking for a face that shows compassion, strength, and courage," I suggested. "I can't imagine a tougher job than being one of those Civil War nurses."

She shook her head dismissively. "Anyway, he's pretty incredible. Not who I expected to run into out here in the hills."

I chuckled. "He's one of the richest guys in the county. He gets six-figure commissions for each of those paintings and probably averages three a year."

"What does he do with the money?"

"Supports his parents who are both at the assisted living center in town. Sponsors a pretty active art program in the school district. The rest he just squirrels away. The guy's got everything . . ."

Before I could finish the thought, the air cracked with a report from a large caliber rifle. The trunk of a small sassafras six feet beyond my open window exploded in a shower of shredded bark and wood.

5

While doing village sweeps in Iraq, I'd seen guys move fast, driven by fear and instinct. But I'd never seen anyone move faster than Mara Joseph when the shot shattered the sassafras. The ruts had slowed my descent into the holler to a rocking crawl. With what struck me as a single motion, Joseph swept her weapon from beneath her jacket, threw open the door, and rolled from the squad car into heavy brush that clogged the runoff ditch. Something of a Deputy Ritter move, but with a practiced precision that suggested she's learned it somewhere other than in her back yard.

The shot had jolted my own heart into high gear, but just as quickly I'd recognized it as what it was—the Greaves way of letting us know no one was welcome in their mean-spirited corner of the world. I braked the Explorer to a halt and stepped cautiously out behind the open door. Two angry dogs snarled up from somewhere below.

"Verl," I shouted. "It's me. Sheriff Tate. I need to talk to you and LJ."

"I know who it is," a voice I recognized as Verl's called back from beyond a turn in the lane. "You ain't welcome here, Tate. Can't just come onto a man's property any time you damn well please."

"I can get permission if I need to, Verl. But I don't think you want that. I just need to talk to you. May as well not send me away and have me come back all pissed off and bringing some extra firepower. And you know you've already given me cause. You can't be firing at law enforcement, or anyone else, for that matter, just because they crossed your property line." I was shouting down at the tree line, but could see no one. There was no sign of Joseph on the other side of the car.

"A man's got a right to defend his property. And you know I was just firin' to warn you off. Otherwise I'd a shot you dead. What you want? We ain't got nothin' down here that don't belong to us." Then to the dogs. "Shut up, you damn sons-a-bitches or I'll blow your damn heads off!" The dogs quieted fast enough that they understood and knew he meant it.

"I'm not worried about what you might be stealing, Verl. We've had a death, and I need to ask you some questions about it."

"We ain't shot nobody, neither. Who's been kilt?"

"I didn't say anybody'd been killed. Just that there's been a death I need to talk to you about."

"You wouldn't be comin' out here 'cause someone's dropped over from no heart attack. Who's died?"

"Your neighbor. Nettie Suskey."

There was silence for a long minute. Then, "What kilt her?"

"We don't know. That's why I . . . I want to talk to you and LJ." My voice was wearing out from all the hollering and was starting to break like I was revisiting puberty.

"You think we kilt her?"

"I don't have any idea who killed her. But you're her closest neighbors. I thought you might have seen or heard something that would help."

Another long silence. "Okay. You come on down. But we're watchin' you!"

I walked around the Ford and looked into the drainage ditch. No sign of Joseph. Just matted grass and a few broken branches. And some smashed poison ivy. She must have made her way back up to the road.

I eased the squad car the rest of the way down the hill, scanning the trees and brush on the right for signs of the state investigator. She had disappeared.

The Greaves lived in what could best be described as a bare metal building with two doors in one end: a garage-sized roll-up, and a regular walk-through door with a faded yellow curtain pulled across its single window. Old pickup trucks, tractors, a mid-sized CAT dozer, and rusty lawnmowers covered the ground on three sides, with the bare patch of dirt in front reserved for an engine hoist and a fenced pen that held two red-eyed pit bulls. Verl and LJ stood beside the hoist, the older man with a pump action twelve-gauge shotgun, Verl with what I recognized as a Marlin 336 with a scope. LJ's chest-length beard and grease-stained bib overalls were legend in the county, allowing folks to spot him from across the square and steer clear. Verl's sagging belly stretched his gray, long-sleeved denim shirt down over a matching pair of faded jeans. His head was shaved slick as a cue ball, but he sported a week's growth of dark whiskers.

I climbed slowly from the squad car, keeping my hands where both could see them.

"You boys need to be a little more careful about using those weapons. You don't want me coming down here because you really did shoot someone."

"This is sovereign territory, once you turn off the ridge road," LJ growled. "We have every right to be defendin' it. You saw the sign."

Both men had their weapons resting on their right shoulders, fingers inside the trigger guards. I nodded and tried to look unconcerned, hand close to my own weapon. "I'm not trespassing, and you only have a right to defend yourself if someone's threatening you. I just need a little help from those who live close to Nettie."

"We ain't seen or heard nothin'," Verl growled. "We leave the old woman alone, and she don't come near us."

"Your land butts up with hers along the back. You haven't heard anything unusual over there?"

LJ waved his free arm in the direction of Nettie's trailer. "She's near a half-mile down the creek. Less it was a shot, we wouldn't a heard nothin' here. Somebody shoot the old biddy?"

"I don't think Nettie ever did any harm to anyone, LJ."

"Nor any good, neither," he snorted.

I glanced around at the rusted skeletons of cars and machinery. "You boys doing anything to clear things out before they flood the valley?"

"Suing the sons-a-bitches," Verl snapped. "Ain't right that they can just say they want this land and take it from a man."

"May not be right. But they can do it, Verl. They should be offering you fair market value."

His hand tightened around the stock of the Marlin. "Ain't no fair price for a place like this. It's been our land since Pa's grandpa settled here. And it's got a good fifty thousand dollars-worth of timber. How you gonna value that?"

"You got a point there, Verl. They should be taking that into account. But I'm afraid they can take it." I looked beyond the metal building and junked vehicles to where a scraped clearing still held a stack of walnut saw logs. "I see you been cutting some, and heard you've already taken a couple of loads to the mill."

LJ shuffled uneasily. "If they flood it, we gotta be gettin' what we can from it. Can't be waitin' til they run us off."

"Some of the folks up on the ridge said they hadn't heard any cutting the last few days. You taken what you plan to?"

"We been haulin' logs," LJ growled. "Getting' them over to the mill."

"People also said they'd been hearing logging on the back of Nettie's place. You must have at least heard that."

LJ swung the 12-gauge from his shoulder, the barrel pointed at my feet. "By people, you must mean that spastic little bastard down the road. Hell, he can't hold hisself steady long enough to know what he's hearin'."

"I didn't say who it was, LJ. Just that I'd received a report of logging on the back of Nettie's land."

"You hintin' at something, Tate? Is that why you come down here? Thinkin' we might o' killed the old bitch for her timber?

Well, you can just be getting' your sad ass off this property."

If there were two people in the county I knew would shoot me as soon as spit on me, I was looking at them. I forced what I hoped looked like a relaxed grin and wondered what the hell had happened to Mara Joseph.

"I'm not hinting at anything, LJ. I was just saying that I'd think if anyone was cutting timber on the back of Nettie's place, you'd of heard it. And I didn't see any roads cut in from behind her house. That would mean whoever was cutting must have come in from this end."

Verl eased the Marlin around and pointed it just below my belt, still holding it with one hand. He hadn't chambered a round while I'd been facing them, but I guessed one had replaced the bullet that shattered the sassafras.

"People been known to disappear round here for accusin' people of less than that, Tate. Why don't you just be puttin' that handgun of yours on the ground in front of you. I ain't sure we can be havin' you spreadin' gossip around about us, with Nettie bein' dead."

"Do you think me disappearing's going to keep someone else from coming down here to question you guys? I'm not here to check on Nettie's trees. I'm just trying to find out what happened to the old lady."

"You're just makin' it sound like maybe we had something to do with it," LJ said, pumping a shell into the chamber of the 12-gauge. "You're trespassing on sovereign land that's been posted, and I'd say now we're feelin' threatened."

There's no sound quite as distinctive and quite as disconcerting as that of a pump-action shotgun chambering a round—unless it's the thump and whistle of an incoming IRAM round. I'd been conditioned in Iraq to duck and cover at the sound of a mortar, but I'd walked too far from the squad car to see any good cover if LJ got serious with the shotgun.

There was motion at the corner of the metal building behind the men at the same instant I heard her command.

"Put those weapons down. *Now!*" she ordered. "And if one of you so much as turns, I'll drop you both." For a small woman, the voice was hard as flint and edged with conviction. Both men stood frozen with uncertainty.

"I'd do what she says," I suggested. "She's got a 9-millimeter pointed right at the middle of your back." I didn't indicate whose back.

Verl let the barrel droop, then slowly lowered the rifle to the ground. The old man appeared to relax, then swung awkwardly toward the voice behind him, the shotgun leveled waist high. Joseph's round caught him in the right side as he turned, throwing him sideways after the 12-gauge that bounced harmlessly a yard away.

I swept out my own weapon and trained it on Verl's chest as he bent toward the rifle. "Don't do it, Verl," I barked, and he pulled back.

LJ writhed with enough pain that it was clear his wound wasn't mortal. "Keep Verl covered and I'll see if I can stop up the bleeding," I said to Joseph. "Then you'd better drive up to the ridge road and call for an ambulance."

She skirted the younger man, picked up the rifle and shotgun, and tossed them into the back of the patrol car. LJ was conscious enough to follow her with a string of expletives. "You blew half my side off," he screamed after her, followed by a list of descriptors that hung in the air like blue fog. She returned to Verl, cuffed his hands behind him to a brace of the engine hoist, and holstered her weapon.

"You think you can keep LJ there from beating you unconscious with his good arm while I call this in?" she asked with a cynical grin.

"I think I can handle it," I said. She kept an eye on the three of us as she swung the Ford around in the clearing and gunned it up the hill toward clear reception.

6

Grace came out to drive Verl into the jail. Chase followed in his ambulance to pick up LJ. Two paramedics in a red pumper truck reached the holler about the same time. One rode with Chase in the ambulance to drip a little blood back into the old man during the hour and a half drive to Springfield.

"I've got a 'Do Not Revive' order out on that old bastard," Joseph called to the medic as she slid back into the passenger side of the cruiser. "If you seem to be losing him, let him go."

"Such hostility!" I said with a chuckle. "You'd think you were the one with the barrel pointed at your crotch."

Her dark eyes stared daggers. "What were *you* going to do, Tate? Chat until one of them got worried enough to shut you up?

"They wouldn't have shot me."

"You were looking like you thought they might."

"I was just getting ready to back away. They'd have let me go." I saw no reason to tell her I was considering Frankie's "drop, draw, and roll," maneuver.

"That old man sure as hell was intent on shooting *me*!"

"Yeah, but you surprised him. And you're not from around here. And a woman. Three strikes, all at once. Nice shot, by the way. You brought him down without killing him."

"A foot left of where I intended."

"Good thing. This saves us a coroner's inquest and all kinds of paperwork."

She shook her head. "There will be plenty as it is. What charges do you plan to bring?"

I was driving again and we were turning back onto the ridge road. "Against Verl? None. LJ's going to be stoved up for a few weeks and for your sake, we'll need to charge him with attempted assault. We'll let Verl sit in jail while we check out the logging claim. That's likely to get a judge more riled up around here than LJ turning a gun on you when you were on his place. And you were the one who got off a shot."

"Damn it, Tate. We're law enforcement officers, following up on a homicide lead. And the bastard turned his weapon on me."

"Hey. I'm with you. But we were on posted, private land without a warrant, Joseph. They'd told me to leave. As much as people around here have no room for the Greaves, they have a lot less for people who don't respect their property rights if there's no warrant. And mean as they are, the old boys don't have any history of shooting anybody."

"You don't think he would have shot me?"

"Oh, he would have shot you. But only because you came up behind them with a weapon. Castle doctrine, stand your ground, and all that stuff. Both will say they told me to leave, and you came up with a weapon drawn."

"They were talking like they weren't going to *let* you leave."

"They'd have let me go. They knew other people knew we were at their place."

"You don't think they killed Nettie?"

Now there, I wasn't so sure. If she had caught them cutting her trees and threatened to report them, one might easily have followed her home and suffocated the old woman. "I'm not ready to say that," I confessed. "But we've got a few things to take care of before we do more to follow up." I gave her a quick once-over to estimate the damage. "For one thing, when you bailed from the car back there, you rolled into a patch of poison ivy. I'm going to drop you at my place and you can shower and run your clothes through the wash before you do anything else. And I'd keep your hands off your jacket and pants until we get you cleaned up."

Joseph's hands flew out in front of her like she was about to catch a beachball. She looked down, wide-eyed at her uniform.

I suppressed a smile. "Your hands and face are the only exposed skin. If you got it on you there, you'll probably break out. It needs to be washed off with soap within about fifteen minutes, max. If it's just on your clothes, we can clean them up."

"If it's on my skin, we can't do anything about it now?"

"I've got some stuff that can reduce the rash and itching. But once the oil gets into the skin, it's nasty." She sat for the next five minutes, hands extended and neck stretched away from her collar.

I live in a modest place on fifteen acres of woods overlooking the same stream that flows past the Greaves' and Nettie's place. I'm a good two miles upstream from where they plan to put the dam and, if anything, it's going to be good for me. I figure the creek will be about twice as wide and half again as deep where it flows below the house. Perfect for smallmouth and crappie. The drive is gravel and a quarter-mile long, but I keep it graded and think of it as a nice rustic introduction to my kind of country living.

The house is sided in rough-cut cedar with windows covering the half that opens onto a wide covered deck facing south and overlooking the creek. I don't have much time for yard work and have stuck with a patch of grass in front I can manage in fifteen minutes with a push mower. Hostas and azaleas crowd against the house on the shady north. A path of rust-colored flagstones runs from the concrete pad in front of the garage to the main porch, then around the side and through an arbor of wisteria to steps that climb onto the deck. I heard a light gasp from Joseph as we pulled up.

"What a lovely place!" She didn't sound at all like the gun-toting inspector who had just dropped LJ Greaves.

"Pretty basic," I said. "But it does have a spare room with shower and a pretty good washer and dryer. Why don't you let me come around and let you out. After I get you in the house, I'll wipe down the vehicle."

I led her into the front vestibule and suggested she ease off her jacket and turn it inside out. "I'll take it into town with me and drop it at the cleaners when I go file my reports."

She glanced curiously about the cedar-paneled entryway while she stripped off the jacket, her gaze settling on a painting of two dog-tired Civil War soldiers, one in blue, one gray, collapsed against opposite sides of a broken stone wall.

"One of Darnell's paintings?"

"Yup. One of his early ones."

"Amazing detail. You can see how beat these men are."

"Beat and sad," I agreed. "It's a reminder when I come in each day of the futility of war—and violence in general."

"You're in a strange line of work for a pacifist," Joseph said with a wry grin.

"If we work together very long, you'll see I'm hardly a pacifist. And you can be in this job because you hate violence."

"I guess that's why we're tracking down Nettie's killer," she agreed.

She followed me down a short hall to the spare room and bath on the right, but continued left into the main part of the house. It's basically open, a kitchen and dining area separated from the living room by a waist-high bar of polished walnut, open at both ends. Rustic tile in the eating areas. Tongue and groove oak flooring in the living room. My bedroom and bath go off the living room toward the back, opposite sliding doors that open out onto the deck.

Joseph stopped a step into the kitchen and swept the space with a critical eye.

"Did you design this?"

"I modified a plan I found somewhere. The bar was a wall in the original plan."

"I love it. And these rugs? You brought them back from Iraq?"

"There, Pakistan, and Afghanistan."

"I think of Middle Eastern carpets as being mainly red and black. But these are mostly grays and earth tones."

"They're actually Persian, traded into those other countries.

That one's a Nain." I pointed at an elaborately patterned carpet in creams and browns beneath a rustic walnut coffee table. "And that one's a Tabriz."

"You know a lot about carpets."

"Not really. I got what I liked and learned about them when I got home."

"They look valuable. And I noticed your house wasn't locked."

"What for? If someone wants to break in, they'll break in. I'm a quarter-mile from anyone and four miles out of town. No one would hear an alarm if I had one. Plus, where are you going to fence something like these rugs? They'd steal the coffeemaker and TV."

She headed for the doors out onto the deck.

"Would you mind giving your hands a good scrub before you start touching everything? That's why we came by here. Remember?"

She detoured to the sink, pushed the faucet arm up with an elbow, and squirted soap onto one hand with the other wrist. While she scrubbed, I wiped down the faucet she'd just contaminated and the top of the soap dispenser, then slid open the sliding doors to save her the trouble. She stepped out onto the deck, drying her hands on a paper towel. The slope dropped away steeply to the creek below, leaving an open view of a wide pasture beyond that filled the rest of the valley.

"Is that your land on the other side?"

"No. I just go to the creek. But that's flood plain. It gets covered every spring, so I don't worry about anyone building there. Old Hank Pethybridge cuts it for hay."

"So beautiful," she murmured. "I could use some of this peacefulness at the end of a day."

"And what do you have instead?"

"A second floor apartment just off Park Central Square, if you know the city. Convenient. Nice places to eat. Hardly quiet. And no view."

"Well, when you get cleaned up, you can come out here and unwind. Why don't you go into the spare room, toss your clothes out and I'll run them through the wash, then head into town and get things filed while you shower and run them through the dryer. You'll find a robe in the closet. I'll leave some lotion on the kitchen counter to rub into your hands, neck and face as soon as you get showered. If you got the oil on your skin, it should help reduce the reaction."

She turned back onto the house. "Do you want *all* my clothes?"

"Up to you. But I'm not separating whites. Everything goes in the same batch. Warm wash and rinse."

She disappeared into the spare bath while I found the lotion in my own bathroom cabinet. When I came back to the bedroom door, all of her clothes were in a loose pile outside. No whites. But some pale pinks. I couldn't resist pausing for a moment to envision the lithe body I could hear splashing under the shower head just two closed doors away. It was the first time a naked woman had graced the premises.

"Did you find the robe?" I shouted.

The shower ended. "Yes. Thank you."

"I'm out of here then. Make yourself at home. Be sure to put some of the lotion on any skin that was exposed. I'll be about two hours."

"I expect you'll find me on the deck."

"There's beer in the fridge. You're welcome to anything else you can find. We can decide where we go from here."

"Gotcha," she called, and I left while I still had the resolve.

7

It took the two hours I'd estimated to get the paperwork filed, drop Joseph's jacket at the cleaners, stop by the courthouse to ask Judge Werner for a couple of warrants, and call people Joseph might want to visit during the afternoon. She'd get a much better reception if I let them know a woman state officer might be coming by and was an alright person.

When I got to the office, Grace had delivered Verl to Rocky for safe keeping and gone back out to check on a report that a cougar had been spotted roaming the Zeorlin farm. The big cats are just starting to show up in the state and every time one crosses someone's land, we get a call. Marti had a couple of messages waiting, one that didn't need attention until tomorrow and one that added another complication to my day.

"The crime lab called," she said after I'd finished my report and handed it to her to file.

"You've waited until now to tell me?"

"I didn't want to put you in a foul mood before you got your paperwork finished. You hate it enough as it is."

I slumped into a chair across the desk from her, wondering what news could be worse than that Nettie's death was a murder, which I knew already. "Okay. Hit me with it."

Marti Bleasdale has been with the department through three sheriffs, about fifteen deputies, and half-a-dozen mayors. Even if she weren't the perfect administrative assistant, her institutional memory would be worth keeping her around. But she's smart, discreet, completely loyal if you do your job and keep things on the up-and-up, and knows more about what's going on in town than anyone but Jerry at the market. She'd been mainly responsible for turning in the last sheriff and half his staff when they started sharing the take with a meth lab that had sprung up on the east side of the county.

"I can't abide using the public trust to break the law," she told the court, then swore that Grace, Rocky, and Bobby Lule hadn't known anything about it. And she'd accepted the new sheriff as her personal project, believing she could turn me into "what this county really deserves."

"From the prints we sent to Springfield, they were able to identify four people," she announced. "One set they can't match."

"Who did they identify?

"Nettie's, of course. And one set was Reverend Latimer. He had prints on file from his time in the service and from some deal the church does that includes anyone who works with kids. His prints were on the arms of another chair in the living room. The third set belonged to Brenda Castoe."

"She had prints on file?"

"Yeah. She'd been through the TSA Pre-Check process. Her prints were several places in the living room and kitchen."

"I guess that shouldn't surprise us. She said she gets by there every few weeks. Do we know anything about the one's they can't identify?"

"There were a couple of partials. They were just on the screen door. Like maybe someone pulled the door open, then decided to put gloves on or not touch anything else. Nothing in the trailer looked like it had been wiped down. They aren't sure if they're a man's or a woman's. But they don't show up in any of the databases."

"Do we know that the Greaves have print records?"

"Yes. Both. These weren't theirs. But they did get a match on the blood and skin under Nettie's nails. That's the bad news."

Yes. Things *could* be worse. I could learn they belonged to Darnell Budgeon or some other citizen I really cared about. I sucked in a breath. "And . . .?"

"They were hers. You don't have any DNA of the murderer."

"They were hers? She scratched herself?"

"She had some sores on her legs that she'd been scratching at. There's nothing to indicate she scratched her killer."

"Damn," I muttered and pushed out of the chair. "Tell Grace when she comes back that she doesn't need to print Verl or check him for scratches. And call Springfield and tell them the same for LJ."

"Grace knows," Marti said. "But she and Rocky already made Verl strip. I suggest we don't tell him we learned this. He's mad as a trapped polecat as it is."

"Won't hear it from me," I promised and headed for the cleaners.

When I got back to the house, Joseph was stretched out in a lounge chair on the deck, still in the bathrobe. She looked up with a grin as I stepped through the sliding doors.

"Not what you were expecting? Sorry, but I'm not going back out with a shirt that isn't pressed. I looked in every closet and couldn't find an iron."

"Not every closet. It's on the shelf in the master bedroom, just above the ironing board."

"I didn't feel right poking around in your room."

"I appreciate that. I'll get it for you, and you can iron while I get us some lunch."

She pushed out of the chair and padded barefoot back into the living room. "I already had a sandwich—and there's one for you in the fridge. You need new lettuce. What you have is pretty limp. I also used the last of your tomatoes."

"Did you make a list?" I said with a chuckle, following her into the house.

"As a matter of fact, yes. It's there on the kitchen island. I did put spicy mustard on your sandwich, but no mayo. Hope I guessed right."

I'd gone into the bedroom for the iron and had to shout back into the kitchen. "Good read! Am I that transparent, or are all guys spicy mustard and no mayo?"

"I think maybe all guys who live in cedar houses with carpets on the floor they brought back from Iraq," she called back. Pretty damned perceptive.

I set up the board beside the kitchen island, plugged in the base for the cordless iron, and retrieved the sandwich and a light beer. She ironed, and I ate while I ran through the rest of my morning.

"I've got a warrant for the Greaves place and one that will allow us access to any bank accounts Nettie might have through the branch. I'll run you back to your car, and thought I'd go check out the report the Greaves were poaching timber, then stop by the bank to see if she had an account. If she has a will, Able Pendergraft probably drew it up. She wouldn't have trusted one of the two young lawyers in town. Able's office is on the square opposite the front doors of the courthouse. Pendergraft and Sumner. Do you need to get back to Springfield to file a report on the shooting?"

She lifted the shirt to see if the collar folded over the way she wanted it to. There was something comfortably domestic about the whole scene and I found I liked it.

"I called my troop commander," she said. "Told him about the shooting, and that we had a little more work to do down here this afternoon. I can file the report when I get back tonight."

I finished off a pickle slice and started on the second half of my sandwich. "Why don't you start with Pendergraft and check on a will. Then go visit with Jerry Covell at Family Market. He needs to get to know you. See how Nettie bought her groceries. Like you said, it's a bit strange that we didn't find anything at the house related to Social Security, Medicare, or savings accounts. In fact, you might also check in at the clinic and talk to Doc Waterman's receptionist. I can't imagine she hasn't been in there for something. Be good to know how she paid her bills."

The thump and shush of the iron had stopped. I looked up from my last bite which was, I had to admit, better than anything I ever made at home. Joseph had put the shirt aside and was stretching her jeans out on the board.

"You iron your jeans?"

"I saw you looking at them when I first arrived this morning. It wasn't because they were wrinkled."

I grinned over at her. "You're right. I admit it was the fit I was appreciating."

"The *pressed* fit," she corrected.

"Oh, right. The pressed fit. But back to this afternoon. Family Market is a block off the square to the east.

She cradled the iron, carefully picked up the shirt and pressed jeans, and disappeared down the hall to the spare room. I heard her hanging the robe in the closet. Within two minutes, she was back at the table as if this was something she did at every first lunch.

"I assume you have warrants for the doctor's records and for the attorney's office to see the will." She slid into a chair opposite me.

"If Nettie has a will, we'll get a warrant. No reason to add to the judge's load if there's no will. And I'm not asking to look at medical records. Just find out how she paid."

"Technically, that may also require a warrant. HIPAA's about as fussy as any set of laws we work with."

I shrugged. "Nancy will tell me. It can't compromise Nettie's privacy for me to know how she paid her bills."

"If you have to ask, it compromises her privacy. I thought you were telling me people were all about privacy and personal rights around here."

"They're also about helping out, especially when one of their own people's been killed." I leaned over and examined her neck. "Did you get that lotion on everything that might have been exposed?"

She held out her hands and turned them in front of me. "Everything except my hair. And I double washed it. I'm not feeling any itching."

"Did you clean your weapon?"

"Very thoroughly."

"Have you ever had it before? Poison ivy?"

She shook her head.

"Then if you got it, it's going to be a few days before it shows up. You'll know it if it does. Ugly rash and itches like the devil." I looked down at my empty plate. "And by the way, great sandwich."

"One of my specialties." She glanced at a black Apple watch on her wrist. "If we're going to catch places before they close, we'd better get moving."

"I've got a couple of chops in the fridge. Let's meet here after we make our visits and compare notes. I'll grill them outside so it doesn't get too warm in here." I smiled over at her. "You're going to be at the market. Why don't you pick up what we need for a salad? You have the list."

"I can't be too late starting back."

"You'll have to have dinner somewhere," I said, and guided her back out to the patrol car.

I deposited Joseph at her Tahoe in front of Nettie's doublewide and drove back over to see what the Greaves had been up to. She followed me up onto the ridge road, then turned toward town to see if the old woman had a will and to try to find out how she paid her bills.

Property lines in this part of the state are kept as much in shared memory as in public record. Everyone could tell you that the line between Nettie's property and the Greaves runs just west of the spring that bubbles out of the base of the hill on the south side of the valley, creating the little brook that runs by her trailer before flowing into the creek. A barbed wire fence had once separated the properties, maybe two or three paces west of the spring. It had long since been flattened by falling branches and the weight of multiflora rose that climbed, then crushed anything it could get its tendrils about. There was an iron pin there somewhere marking the corner. But the families had owned the property for so long no one had reason to look for it. Neither ran cattle, so keeping a fence in good shape didn't seem all that important.

A dozer track cut through the trees behind the Greaves' metal building in the direction of the spring. I stopped where I knew the old fence line once ran, not wanting to drag some hidden wire up over an axle. But I could see what I needed to see from where I sat. Two or three acres in front of me had pretty well been clear-cut, with anything over sixteen inches harvested and smaller trees knocked over as trunks fell and logs were dragged back behind the dozer.

With the spring keeping the ground wet, this had been prime bottomland for walnut, ten or more mature trees to the acre. And I could see the limbs of half as many white oak stacked in brush piles across the stripped land. The old boys must have figured Nettie was too deaf to know how close the sound was, would never make it back here to look, and no one else would be prowling this part of the hollow before it got flooded.

I pulled off my boots and climbed onto the hood of the cruiser. With my phone, I took a long sweeping video, starting where the spring rose and making a full 360-degree turn, narrating as I went. "I'm parked on the fence line between the Greaves and Suskey properties, looking east onto Nettie's land. I came down here with a warrant, based on reports that people up on the ridge had heard logging going on that sounded like it was on the Suskey land. As you can see, about three acres have been pretty well clear-cut on the Suskey side, with the only dozer track heading back toward the Greaves. There's been some cutting on the Greaves property behind me, but most has been walnut along the creek bottom. There are logs back beside their house. I'll make a count, then check with the mills around to see where the Greaves have been selling their cut logs and try to get a total. Most of what's been taken recently has come from Nettie's property."

I clambered off the hood, pulled on the boots, then sat for ten minutes wondering if the two worthless sonsabitches would have killed the old woman over this. Of course they would, if she'd confronted them. But it wasn't like Nettie to drive her old jeep down into the back of Blackjack Holler to face off with the Greaves. And if she'd complained to anyone else, I'd have heard about it from Jerry.

I swung the Explorer around, drove back to the building, and made a count of the stacked logs, jotting down the number of walnut and white oak. With the squad car back up on the ridge road, I sent a copy of the video to my email and to Grace's, then gave the deputy a call.

"I know you searched Verl for scratches," I said when she answered, "but let's get a DNA swab while we've got the both of them, in case some trace shows up on her clothes or somewhere.."

"You think they did it?" Grace asked.

"They did a lot of cutting on her place. So they had reason. I just sent you a video to put in the evidence vault. And God knows they're mean enough."

Grace grunted. "I hope they did. I'd love to have some reason to send them both away for as long as either of them's alive."

"Right now," I admitted, "they've got to be at the top of our list."

8

When I reached home, Joseph hadn't returned. Maybe she'd decided she needed to get that shooting report in and had driven back to Springfield. But I didn't judge her to be the type to leave town without letting me know what she'd found.

I'd been keeping a couple of pork chops in the meat saver, threw them in a plastic bag with some marinade, and fired up the grill. If she'd skipped on me, I could probably manage both on my own.

I'm a traditional old charcoal type when it comes to grilling. No self-starting briquettes. Just a chimney starter and a sprinkling of soaked hickory chips for flavor. I was spreading the coals out across the grill when I heard her pull into the drive. She gave two quick knocks and walked on in, coming straight through to the deck.

"Looks like you counted on me staying for dinner," she said, lifting the foil cover off the plate of chops.

I grinned. "Or I've worked up an appetite."

She dropped the foil back over the meat. "Which is it? I'll be getting on the road if I need to get back into fast food land by seven."

"I was thinking of tossing up a salad to go with these. If you want to skip fast food, you can help with that. And there's a pretty good California Merlot in the rack in the island."

She unbuckled her weapon and hung it over the back of one of the porch chairs. "I've had an interesting afternoon and may as well help you with that second chop while we talk. I saw most of the salad fixings when I was making up the sandwiches so should be able to find them again."

I laid the chops on the hottest part of the grill with a pair of tongs, clicked the timer on my phone for three minutes to braise the sides, and followed her back into the house. "I'll get some plates set. In here, or out on the deck?"

Joseph nodded back toward the deck.

"My choice too. It's going to be a nice evening." I flipped a switch just inside the deck door that turned on the bug zapper and started gathering up placemats and silverware.

"Perfectly done," Joseph complimented as she savored her first bite of pork. "What's your secret?"

I poked at my own chop with a fork. "Choice cuts. Jerry butchers all his own meats and cuts these up specially for me. Buys from farmers around who field-raise their hogs. Which brings us around to business. What did Jerry have to tell you?"

Joseph sipped at her wine and dabbed at the corner of her mouth with a napkin. I was enjoying looking across at her. When on the job, she reminded me of a hunting bobcat: compact, quick, and constantly alert. But as she sat across from me, she was the refined city girl: elbows off the table, napkin in her lap, and cutting only one piece of her meat at a time. And she was damn pretty.

She returned the napkin to her lap. "That Jerry is a character! And treated me like we'd always known each other. Like you said, he seems to know everything that goes on about town. Nettie always used cash, both at the market, and everywhere else. Jerry said he'd never seen her use a credit card or check. Always cash. And if she was buying much, she often used hundred dollar bills. New bills."

"He never cashed a check for her? The folks over at the bank said she didn't have an account there and didn't cash checks. The market's pretty much the only other place around town a body can cash a check."

"No. She always had the money she needed. And like I said, often laid out a fresh hundred dollar bill."

"How about a will? Had Able drawn one up for her?"

"He wasn't in. The receptionist thought he'd be in court most of the day, but was pretty sure he'd helped Nettie with one. She was nervous about looking through the files without his approval, even with the warrant. But she promised to have him call when he got back."

"Doesn't seem like that would have taken much of your afternoon. How did you fill the rest of your day?"

She smiled in a way that let me know she didn't feel the need to account for her time. "First of all, you don't have a brief conversation with Jerry Covell. But when I finished with the law office, I walked around your lovely little square seeing what other merchants could tell me about Nettie and her buying habits. Turns out Jerry was absolutely right. She *always* used cash. Usually smaller bills, but sometimes the hundreds he told me about. But the most interesting visits were with the clinic and her minister."

"Bill Latimer?"

"Yes. Loved the guy. He seems the perfect small town pastor. Knew everyone in town and was especially fond of Nettie. He'd been called by the coroner and was pretty shaken—partly by her death, but especially by the fact that she'd been murdered."

"Yeah. He's quite a fixture here. I guess the Methodists try to move their pastors about every seven years or so. Bill refused to be reassigned. I think he's no longer *official* Methodist, but nobody here cares. He preaches a good sermon, runs a good youth program, and takes good care of his parishioners. That's about all anyone wants from their minister. What did he have to tell you?"

Joseph had taken another bite of meat and waited until she had completely finished with it and taken another sip of wine before answering. "Hundred dollar bills. Every first Sunday like clockwork, she left a new hundred in an envelope in the plate."

I started with a question, but she cut me off. ". . . and get this! Your doctor's receptionist—Waterman, if I remember right—said Nettie never applied for Medicare. The woman didn't think she'd ever even applied for Social Security. She didn't come in often, but when she did . . ." She waited expectantly for me to finish the thought.

". . . she paid with new hundreds."

"*Bingo*."

She had answered the question I was about to ask. Whether she'd stopped by Waterman's clinic. But she'd raised a lot more.

"If she's not getting Social Security and not cashing other checks somewhere, where's this cash coming from?"

Joseph had relaxed back into her chair. "What did you learn? Maybe she was selling timber."

It hadn't occurred to me that the Greaves could be cutting *for* Nettie and giving her cash. The mills all liked to deal in cash to keep their financial transactions as fuzzy as possible. But the Greaves hadn't had a good thing to say about Nettie when we confronted them in Blackjack Holler and would have told us about selling for her if it had gotten us off their land.

"I don't think so," I guessed. "They've been cutting a lot of her trees. Probably thousands of dollars-worth. But I didn't get the impression from our little conversation that it was for shares. And she seems to have had money a lot longer than they've been cutting her timber."

"Maybe that woman with the emergency alert system will have some idea where she gets the cash. Other than Reverend Latimer, she seems to have been her most regular contact."

"Brenda Castoe?"

Her answer was interrupted by strains of the Scott Joplin rag that had been used as the theme for the movie "The Sting."

"Sorry," she said, reaching over to her handbag that sat on one of the spare table chairs. "My phone. Maybe that's our attorney."

"Officer Joseph," she said officially, then listened, nodding to let me know it was Able Pendergraft.

"Yes," she said after a moment. "I would appreciate getting a copy. But for now, can you tell me who the beneficiary is and if there are any unusual assets?"

As she listened, a wry smile crept across her animated face as it returned again to bobcat.

"Thank you, Mr. Pendergraft," she said. "Either Sheriff Tate or I will come by and get a copy. Probably tomorrow. But this has been extremely helpful." She ended the call with a satisfied grin.

"Speak of the devil. Who do you think is beneficiary to Nettie's estate, such as it is?"

My mind ran quickly through the names that had come up in the last twenty minutes. Pendergraft? Latimer? Workman? Greaves? I settled on the one who had given Nettie the most support.

"Reverend Latimer and the church," I guessed.

"*Merrrnk!*" She imitated the sound of the buzzers that signal a wrong gameshow answer. "The *other* person who gave her regular attention. Brenda Castoe."

I'd been using the phone conversation to catch up on my own chop and spent the next minute finishing a bite as Joseph had done, mulling over what I'd just heard.

"It will be interesting to find out if she's aware of that bit of information," I offered finally.

"That trailer can't be worth much."

"No. But three hundred acres of prime timber that's about to be purchased through eminent domain is."

"How much?"

"I'd guess the trees can be harvested for tens of thousands of dollars. And the land without them will be valued at three to five thousand an acre."

"That little? Five thousand an acre? Whew! I need to invest in some property down here."

"That's what timberland is generally selling for. And this is going to be flooded, so won't bring top dollar."

"Yes. But that's still hundreds of thousands."

I nodded. "Enough to be a motive."

"Before I drive down from Springfield tomorrow, I'll stop and visit with Mrs. Castoe," Joseph suggested.

"I'd like to be with you."

"You may want to come up for another reason." Joseph gave me her best bobcat grin. "The will says she *does* have a bank account. Well, a safe deposit box. But it's in Springfield. I think you may want to be with me when I open it."

9

I've been surprised in this new job at how often my sense of duty and my personal desires run headlong into each other. Like with the Greaves. Even before I saw how much timber they'd taken off Nettie's land, my personal desire was to go down to their place and whup up on the pair until one of them gave me a reason to shoot him in self-defense. But duty told me that as convinced as I was that Darnell was right, that they didn't have an ounce of goodness between them, they deserved the protection of the law until proven guilty of one of their endless offenses. My assistant Marti would be disappointed in her protégé if I denied the worthless pair due process.

There's a town up in the northwest corner of the state called Skidmore that's become something of a legend in Missouri. Decades ago, back in the early 1980s, the local folk became so frightened and fed up with a town bully that the man was gunned down by snipers on Main Street while sitting in his truck. Twenty-five or thirty people saw the shooting, but no one ever talked. One of those unsolved crimes that people would just as soon remain unsolved. Well, that's pretty close to how I felt about the Greaves. If someone happened to find that pair dead in their junk warehouse someday, I'd have a hard time investigating it very enthusiastically.

But on this particular night, admiring Inspector Mara Joseph as she sipped at her wine across the table, the personal desire that bumped up against good professional judgment was to suggest that she not drive back to Springfield, but stay with me and drive up in the morning. I'd suggest the spare room, of course. Then hope that some overpowering chemical attraction would bring one of us to the other's door during the night and we'd end up awkwardly explaining to the other that it really wasn't like us to mix pleasure with business. But it *shouldn't* be like us. So I savored the thought for a few minutes, hoping she was having the same fantasy and might be less resolute, then said what duty required.

"Do you know any judges well enough to call one this late? It would be nice to get to that box as soon as the bank opens. If it gives us some clue as to where Nettie's money came from, I'd like to have that bit of information in hand when we talk to Brenda Castoe."

"There's one I can call." She showed just enough hesitation that I wondered if she'd been harboring the same fantasy. "I knew him in law school and we dated a few times. I'll call him now and see if I can swing by and get a warrant when I get up there this evening." She hesitated. "You know, if we want to start early, it would make sense for you to follow me up and bunk in my spare room tonight. It would cut an hour off your morning."

Ah! The stars must be aligned! "Wouldn't your neighbors talk?" I asked with a chuckle.

"My neighbors don't pay much attention to me. And if they're talking about me, they won't be talking about someone else." She fixed me with a gaze over the wine bottle. "And this is a business invitation, so they'll have nothing to talk about."

"Of course," I said. "And one I'll accept." I stood from the table and began gathering up dishes. She picked up her own glass and plate and headed for the sink.

"Anyway, I ran into that deputy of yours while I was in town this afternoon. What's her name? Grace? A very pretty woman, and she wasn't wearing a ring. My guess is that you're used to a little gossip."

I was, and if Grace didn't have a serious boyfriend, there would have been good reason for it. If I was ranking Joseph as a six on the Richter scale of good looks, Grace was about one point short of a full nine. She doesn't wear the makeup that would make her look stunning and is so damn professional it forces me to be the same. But if she wanted to, and decided to get her hair out of that ponytail she sticks through the back of her ball cap, she'd rattle every window between here and St. Louis. None of that kept people around town from talking, especially over at *A Cut Above* on weekday mornings.

"Yeah. She's a pretty one," I confessed, "but is all business and has a guy who guards her like a sheepdog."

"And you've chosen not to share this lovely little spot with anyone else?" She deposited the dishes at the sink and crossed to the bar that separated the kitchen from the living room, picking up a picture of me with Adeena. Yellowstone's Morning Glory pool steamed in vivid turquoise and orange in the background. "And this is another lovely woman."

"The closest I've come to having a housemate."

"You still display the picture."

"Not too many people come in here. It's mainly there for me. Am I being interrogated?"

She replaced the picture and looked around the room for other clues of who she was working with and who she had just invited home. Another photo showed me with Adeena in front of the Sultan Qaboos Grand Mosque in Muscat.

Joseph turned to me with a questioning smile. "She's Arab?"

"Was," I said simply. "Her family is Palestinian." I watched Joseph for a reaction.

"She changed her faith?"

"No. She was killed a few years ago."

"Oh. I'm so sorry," she said, showing nothing but sincerity. "What happened to her, if I might pry a little?"

Mere thought of that afternoon quickened my pulse and tightened the muscles along my jaw. "One of the many Bagdad suicide bombings. This one at a hotel."

"*Hmm*," Joseph murmured. "Every person in the Middle East's worst nightmare. Were you there at the same time?"

The memories that had tightened the jaw now forced beads of cold sweat onto my temples and upper lip. I wiped the side of my brow with a hand that shook more than I wanted her to see.

"We were in the city at the same time, but not at the same functions. She went to interpret for a visiting group at a hotel in the city. I took a party at the embassy inside the Green Zone I thought might win me a few political points. Worst decision of my life." My voice showed the same tremor.

Joseph looked back at the photo. "Were you married?" she asked quietly.

I sucked in a deep breath. "About to be. We met while working in the embassy in Bahrain. Both doing interpreting work. She was from Chicago. Second generation American. And because of my time in Iraq and Afghanistan, I knew more about that part of the world than she did. She helped me polish my Arabic. I helped her get used to desert life and being more careful about where she went as a single woman." The memories prompted a melancholy smile. "To begin with, I volunteered to be her male escort when she wanted to drive over into Dammam or Riyadh. Before we knew it, we were a serious couple."

"How long ago did this happen?" She lifted the picture of the two of us in Muscat and studied it more carefully.

"Two years next month."

"She is lovely," she said softly, then turned with a questioning smile. "So you escaped back into the hills?"

"You don't escape something like that. You just gradually learn to manage it."

"And you don't risk it again." It was more a statement than a question.

I hesitated, surprised I'd let the conversation go this far, but realizing I wanted her to know. "Not in any serious way. Not yet, at least."

She replaced the photo onto the side table. "That should make you the ideal house guest," she quipped. "Why don't you grab what you'll need and I'll call Judge Lindstrom. I'll give you a key and an address. If he can draw something up for us tonight, I'll stop and pick it up and meet you at my place."

"I need to call Grace. Let her know I'll be in Springfield for at least the morning." I headed for the bedroom, knowing that after the discussion we'd just had, there was going to be no irresistible chemistry and no late-night door knocking. Probably as it should be.

10

Any remaining fantasies of a midnight rendezvous were jarred away by a sharp rap on the door and a "Tate, we'd better get moving if we're going to be at the bank when it opens." I glanced at a bedside clock and bailed from the bed. Seven-fifteen blinked back at me. I'm an early riser. Generally up and having my microwave bowl of oatmeal with brown sugar, blueberries, and shelled walnuts by a quarter of six. But I sometimes find that worrisome problems and being reminded of half-buried tragedies keep me awake late, then sap away the normal energy that rousts me out early.

Joseph and I had talked over a glass of wine until 11:00, briefly about what we knew about Nettie's murder, then at length about how I'd gotten into interpreting.

She was lounging in the corner of her sofa and, after a long, inquisitive look, asked, "After driving around your home turf, how in the world did you get into Middle Eastern languages, Tate? It's sort of like leaving there to become a ballet dancer or something."

I grinned at her over my glass. "And the reaction was about the same. But I told you about my reading obsession. I'd come across these foreign phrases in what I read and had to look them up. It was a bit like solving puzzles, with these strange symbols representing words and ideas. I felt like I had to understand them."

"You couldn't have picked many things more difficult—especially in the language category."

A broader grin. "I could have gone into Asian languages. But I preferred learning a new alphabet rather than sets of symbols that represent words or phrases. I started with an on-line course in

Arabic my senior year of high school, loved it, and used it to finagle my way into American University in DC. I think their admissions people said, 'We've got to see this kid from the Ozarks who's studying Arabic.' I joined the Marines after graduation. Went through the defense language school in Monterey, and you know the rest of the story."

"Except how you ended up in Bahrain."

Not somewhere I'd wanted the evening to go. But we were relaxed, I wanted her to feel comfortable with me, and this was probably part of getting there. "I joined the State Department when discharged, managed to get assigned to the Bureau of Near Eastern Affairs, and was assigned to Language Services. My first assignment was the embassy in Oman. Then I was moved to Bahrain and ran into this beautiful Arab-American from Chicago. I wouldn't say it was love at first sight, but for me, it was love during the first month. It took her a little longer."

She waited silently, indicating she wanted to hear the explanation.

"Her family. I wasn't what they'd hoped for in a partner for their daughter. Not Muslim. Not Palestinian. Not even a sophisticated city boy."

"But she didn't let that get in her way?"

"She was like you in that respect. Bullheaded and *very* much her own person." Joseph's wry smile suggested she wasn't sure if she'd just been complimented or insulted.

"And I gather you were both transferred to Iraq."

Again I felt the flush and tightening in my face. "Sent on loan. There were a couple of big functions going on in Baghdad, and they needed a bunch of interpreters. I knew the assignment inside the Green Zone was the most secure, but I talked her into taking the hotel assignment because . . ." I had to finish the sentence with a silent blinking stare into the cushions between us.

She reached over and laid a hand on mine. "I'm so sorry, Tate. You couldn't have known. But thank you for sharing a little of her with me. Time to turn in. We have an early appointment."

I'd stared at the ceiling in her spare room until about 1:00 a.m., re-living hearing the sound of the explosion from the courtyard of the Embassy, and knowing in my gut where it came from and what it meant. While the Marine guards hustled all of the important dignitaries back into secure rooms in the building, two of the news people and another interpreter rushed with me to the rubble that had once been the hotel. I could see as soon as we turned onto the street that no one had survived. I had flown home with what they could identify as Adeena's body and had endured three days of her family's wrath. It was another year before I had a night that wasn't haunted by dreams of explosions and angry parents and sending her into harm's way.

In Joseph's spare room I tried to shut out the memories by turning to Nettie's case and troubling over whether I was overlooking something there that a better sheriff might think of. If I've got a major personality flaw, it's probably that I overthink. Adeena liked to say that I try to anticipate every possible problem that might come my way, no matter how unlikely, and work out a solution in advance for each—just in case. The habit served to keep me out of serious trouble a couple of times while in the service, but it consumes a good bit of time and stresses me about things that don't deserve the worry. And it didn't keep me from sending Adeena to that hotel rather than letting her take the safer embassy party. Last night had been one of those nights I'd thought about both Nettie and Adeena until I finally wore my brain out.

Joseph had coffee ready with a box of granola, blueberries, and some kind of Greek yogurt laid out as if this was how everyone started their day. I decided the yogurt would tide me over until lunch, and I'd seen a DQ not far from her apartment. When noon rolled around, I'd stop for a bacon double cheeseburger and medium turtle Blizzard while she found an Asian salad somewhere.

We were in the door of the main branch of Central Ozark Bank so quickly after the manager opened it that I saw him nod toward his security man. I showed him my badge, and Joseph flipped open her credentials, handing the man her warrant.

"We're investigating a murder and need access to the victim's safe deposit box," she explained as the nervous banker studied the document. "We're hoping it may cast light on her sources of income and what kinds of assets she has.

"And have a look at her box access log," I added, not convinced that Joseph needed to be giving the man so much information. The manager waved his guard over to accompany us into the vault where he thumbed through a manual index until he found Nettie's card. For a moment he looked flustered, then handed me a pen.

"I'll need to have one of you sign in to show that the box was accessed," he said. "And I don't know if this authorizes you to take anything from it."

"How about if we just inventory it, photograph anything of interest, and subpoena its contents later if we feel it might be important evidence," Joseph offered. Again, I wasn't sure she needed to be so damned accommodating. But this was her town.

"That would be quite acceptable," the manager agreed and handed me a key. Like two missile officers about to launch a nuclear strike, we inserted our keys into box 211, turning them in unison.

"You can look at it privately over here." The manager slid the long metal box out of its slot and led us to what looked like a curtained voting booth. As he lowered it onto a waist-high marble shelf, something metallic slid within the box.

"Replace it when you've finished, and return both keys to me," the banker said and retreated from the vault, leaving the security guy pinned to a wall near the door.

Joseph looked at me expectantly. "Looks like they want to make sure we don't take anything," she whispered. "This is your case. Have a look."

The only items visible beneath the lid that covered only the front half of the box were a folded sheet of paper torn from a spiral notebook and a yellowed envelope. I slipped on a pair of cotton gloves, lifted out the notebook page, and opened it so both of us could read the hand-scratched message:

> This is what I've pretty much been living on these past years. They seem to be worth more every year. Whoever gets them, be smart about how you use them. From what I hear, they may be all that's left.

I looked over at Joseph who arched a curious brow but waited for me to retrieve the envelope. The aged paper was thick against my fingers and felt as if it might crumble if squeezed or bent. I laid it on the shelf beside the box, gingerly lifted an edge that had long ago been carefully sliced along the top, and slid out two double-folded sheets. The letter paper had survived much better than its container and easily unfolded. I flattened it against the countertop. The writer's hand showed a trace of palsy, but was otherwise better schooled in penmanship than was Nettie's.

> August, 1910
>
> My Dear Son Ruben:
> I have put off writing this a good sight too long, but must now while the breath of life still abides within me. I will be locking it away in the drawer of the old writing desk, knowing you or your brother will find it when I have passed over to whatever awaits.

That will be soon enough. I do not wish you to bear this burden any longer than need be. But I have never had the courage to make amends and must leave it to you to decide what, if any, are required.

You know that I was a soldier for the Union in the great war that divided our country. We had come to the mountains from Pennsylvania and had no tolerance for slaves nor slaveholders. At the end of the war, I was with General James Wilson when we sacked the city of Columbus in Georgia. We left nothing standing or moving and that alone has eaten at my soul. After it was all over, I cannot say that I was truly mustered out. I pretty much walked away, overburdened by the weight of the guilt. Five of us wandered north looking for friendlier territory when we heard the army had captured the South's treasury. Rumor was they was using it to pay off soldiers who hadn't been getting wages. We headed east and caught up with the wagon train that was carrying the loot in Wilkes County, Georgia, but was told there was no pay coming from all that captured money. By then, we was about starved and had another thirty other men with us—some Union, some Reb. Though I had nothing to do with thinking up the plot, next I knew, we had taken the wagons and was passing out the spoils.

I can't say I'm the least proud of what I done and don't hold it up as an example. But all of us grabbed what we could, stole horses from the men guarding the train, and scattered. I'd filled my pockets with enough to keep me alive while I made my way home, and grabbed a canvas bag of coin that I kept in a saddlebag. That I never opened, figuring I'd return it someday if I didn't have need of it. I hid it away and haven't touched it since, though to this day it eats at my soul. I am telling you here where to find it, knowing you to be a sight more honest than your father, and less given to greed and covetousness.

Your weaker self may decide, as I did, that the money didn't belong to the Union government any more than to me. It had been Reb money. I hadn't been paid for most of my time winning that money and deserved to have my share. But this is known to be Reb money. If you show up with it, the government might not be of the same mind. Remember too what the Good Book says about the love of money. I leave all that to you to sort out and to the good Lord who, I fear, has already made a judgment about me.

You will find the bag on the farm in a cleft in the rock where the creek meets the steepest part of the bluff. When the water is low, you can ease along the rock shelf that lies just along the waterline. A shallow ledge, wide as your shoulders, juts out from the cliff chest-high. You will find a slab of rock the size of your mother's old bread *board, but thick as your fist that covers the cleft in the rock. Push it aside and you will find the bag there. Don't let it damn you as I fear it may have damned me.*

Your loving father,
Ezra Suskey

We stood in silence staring at the letter for a full minute after reading the final lines.

"*Wowzer,*" I was finally able to mutter. Joseph started to speak, then shook her head mutely.

"I'm a little concerned about leaving this here," I whispered finally, glancing through the gap in the curtain at the guard. "If this leads to what I think it might, it's going to be a huge temptation to everyone who sees it."

"You mean, like you and me?" Joseph suggested, looking at me darkly.

"I mean, like any investigator or evidence person. We can safeguard it better than anyone else I can think of. I know you know. You know I know. That's pretty good insurance."

"What are you suggesting?"

"Take it back to town and put it in our evidence vault. Rocky keeps a good eye on people messing with evidence, but doesn't worry about what's there."

"You said we wouldn't take anything."

"No. *You* said we wouldn't take anything."

"But I was speaking for both of us."

"I know that. But that was before we knew what anything was."

She clasped her arms across her chest for a long moment,

looking first at me, then at the open box. "I think you're right," she said finally. "But what about this other note?"

I reached a gloved hand back into the box where I had heard something slide. Two disks pressed against the back of the case. I cupped them in my hand and drew them out.

"Oh, my God," Joseph murmured, leaning over the gold coins. "I don't know anything about old money, but I'd say Nettie was right. There's some value in these." I had drawn the money out with a different side showing on each coin. One displayed a woman with shoulder-length hair and an elaborate headdress. Around the edge was "United States of America." The other side was ringed by a flowered wreath, centered by a large "1 dollar," and the date 1861.

"Do you think this is what's left of the stash?" she wondered.

I shrugged. "We'll have to go look. But it's good that these are here. It explains Nettie's note. We photograph these coins with the note and leave them here. If we find more money, we can add it to the vault in Crayton until we get this murder solved. I'd bet two bits to the dollar that whoever killed the woman was after this."

"And thought she was keeping it in the house?

"Or that they could get her to tell them where it's hidden."

"Or . . ." Joseph suggested, ". . . they knew this information was here and just needed Nettie out of the way so it became theirs."

I folded the letter and eased it back into its envelope, slipping it into my inside jacket pocket. Joseph laid the coins beside Nettie's note and snapped half a dozen pictures with her phone, making enough display of it that the guard would notice through the gap in the curtain.

I replaced the items in the box, dropping the lid back in place. Joseph pushed aside the curtain and the guard dislodged himself from the wall.

"All through?"

I nodded, slid the box back into its slot, and turned the keys. We dropped the keys on the manager's desk and thanked him for being so accommodating.

"Did you find anything that will help?" he asked.

Joseph nodded. "There's a note there that could be useful. I've got a photograph. If we need the original, we'll be back with the appropriate paperwork."

"Drop me off at my car," I suggested as we left the bank. "Why don't you get in touch with Brenda Castoe and arrange for her to meet us for lunch. Then go file whatever reports you need to on the box search and get a list of places that might deal in gold or old coins. Let me know where the lunch meeting is and I'll meet you there."

"And you will be doing. . . ?"

I grinned at my inquisitive new partner. "I'll be up at the county library boning up on Civil War gold."

11

When it comes to investigating, the one place I knew I could hold my own with Mara Joseph was the public library. As a high school senior, I'd haunted the Greene County Library for resources the school library didn't have and ordered texts on Arabic that I could only get through the state's vast inter-library network. The reference librarian at the time, a woman named Maggie McKenzie, didn't have kids of her own and saw in me a chance to do some mothering. When I showed up, she always had a stack of articles set aside, and it was her help with my admissions essay that had probably accounted for my getting into American University. Since coming back to Crayton, I had been up to take her to lunch about once a month and sometimes called to seek a little sane advice. She was nearing retirement, but I knew I'd still find her at the reference desk. I also knew she could find some good information about Confederate gold. But I had a couple of more important questions.

She smiled with a delight that I knew was genuine when she saw me across the room, and met me with a warm hug that was always uncomfortably long.

"Colby, you're in your uniform. This must be a business visit," she said, leading me to a quiet table where we could talk privately.

"It's always more than just a business visit, Maggie," I assured her. "But I do need some of your professional help. A woman in Crayton died under suspicious circumstances this week, and I'm investigating. I'm curious about whether you might remember her coming here? It probably would have been five or more years ago."

Maggie's smile was kind, but not encouraging. "You know I see dozens of people every day, Colby. And my memory isn't what it used to be."

"Your memory for names has always amazed me," I flattered. "But I think you would be more likely to remember this woman based on what she would have asked about. Her name is Nettie Suskey. Does that ring a bell?"

She shook her head slowly. "No. I don't recall her."

"Well, I suspect she would have been asking for help on one of two things. Information about old Confederate gold dollars, or about who owns recovered treasure from a Civil War era discovery."

Maggie's eyes narrowed slightly, then she slowly began to nod. "A little lady? She'd be older than I am. Looked like she might not take very good care of herself?"

"That would be her. But very nice and polite. Probably pretty hesitant in the way she asked for help."

Maggie nodded more firmly. "Yes. I remember her. And it was questions about who owned discovered treasure that she wanted help with. I have to admit, Colby, that I thought she was delusional. But she was sweetly delusional, so I did what I could to help her."

"Can you remember when this was?"

"As a matter of fact, it would have been six years ago. I found some articles about a California couple who had found over a thousand gold coins from the early 1800s in their yard. The courts ruled that it was finders, keepers. I know that was six years ago."

I grinned across at her. "I don't think the memory has slipped a bit, Maggie. And that's exactly what I wanted to know."

"Did her death have something to do with a discovered treasure?"

I shrugged. "Hard to say. But I'm concerned that she was *telling* people she'd found something valuable and someone believed her."

Maggie folded her hands on the tabletop and looked at me suspiciously. "And something also told you she might have been up here asking."

"A note we found," I admitted. "It talked about her thinking she knew where some old Confederate gold had been hidden."

Maggie sniffed dismissively. "Those rumors have been flying around for a hundred and fifty years, Colby. But mainly about places on the East Coast. Not Missouri."

I nodded my agreement. "Right. Seems very unlikely. But just for my sake, can you help me find some books or articles about Civil War Confederate gold and what happened to it?"

Her smile told me she had hoped there was more she could do to help. She pushed up from the table. "Stay right here. I'll see what I can find."

12

Two hours later, I was seated with Joseph in a booth at FD's Grillhouse on the south side of the city, waiting for a 12:30 lunch with Brenda Castoe. Joseph said the woman had been visiting clients in Nixa and asked if we could meet her south of the James River Bypass.

"She didn't sound at all concerned on the phone," Joseph said as the waiter brought us both iced tea, Joseph's sweetened and with lemon. "Asked if there was any progress with the investigation and said she was anxious to hear what we knew."

"She was remarkably composed when we found Nettie," I told her. "Said she'd been a hospice nurse and wasn't shaken by much."

Joseph squeezed lemon into her tea. "That would do it. We'll see how she reacts when she learns she's inherited what there is of Nettie's estate." She sipped at the tea and seemed satisfied. "What did you learn about the coins?"

"Well, first of all, I learned Nettie had been to the library to research who would own discovered treasure from that era. She must have been worried about the concern raised in her grandfather's letter."

Joseph lowered her glass to the table and sat back in the booth, her expression puzzled. "And how did you get this little bit of information without a warrant? Library records are usually pretty carefully guarded."

"We each have our sources," I grinned back at her. "I didn't ask to see any records. Just asked the right person if some old lady had come in five or six years ago asking about who might own Civil War gold if it were found. All it took was a simple

'Yes, I remember her.'"

"And someone actually remembered that from five or six years ago?"

"Not only remembered, but could place the year. You don't know librarians like I do."

Joseph arched a brow. "Apparently not. And what did you learn about the coins?"

"I learned that the story in the letter's true. Union forces did commandeer the Confederate treasury and started moving it by wagon train toward Washington. The train was bushwhacked in Wilkes County, Georgia, and much of the loot stolen."

"Then I assume the coins have pretty significant value."

I couldn't suppress a chuckle. "Enough to explain why someone might have a motive for murder. My guess is whoever ransacked the house was looking for those coins, or for something like that letter that would point them to the money."

"Valuable?"

"What do you think they're worth? Take a guess?"

I could tell from Joseph's flicker of a frown that she didn't go for that kind of game, so I didn't wait for her best shot.

"The two in the box are what they call 1861-D or Dahlonega dollars after the mint that produced them. They were the only coins struck exclusively by the South, using some re-purposed 1860 US mint dies. Sometimes they're called Indian Princess dollars for the face of the woman on the front. According to what I read, only 1000 to 1500 were made, making them extremely rare."

Joseph wrinkled her forehead in a way that said, "All very interesting, but what are they worth?"

I gave my own tea a stir with the straw for effect while Joseph took a sip of hers. "And get this. One in mint condition—and the ones Nettie has are primo—sold in 2014 for over $70,000."

Joseph choked into her glass and looked quickly around to make sure no one had overheard me. "*You're kidding*. The two coins in that vault are worth $140,000?"

"I'm just telling you what the one sold for."

"Then she could sell one every couple of years and live pretty comfortably off the cash."

"Which she probably kept in the house—or hidden nearby somewhere."

"I'd say this changes everything."

Since leaving the library, I'd been thinking pretty much the same thing, but wanted Joseph's take on it. "In what way?"

"People around town knew she used cash for all of her purchases. If word got out that she might have a pretty sizable amount stashed in the house, no matter what the source, any lowlife could have come looking for it."

"My thoughts exactly."

"So we've got at least four possibilities." She ticked them off with her fingers against the tabletop. "One: someone knew she might have money in the house and came looking for it. Two: someone learned about the Confederate coins and thought they might be in the house. Three: somebody knew about the letter and wanted to get to the money before the valley gets flooded, so tried to force her to tell where it was hidden. Or, four: the Greaves thought she might turn them in for poaching her timber." Her thumb still remained poised above the table. I reached over and pushed it down.

"Five, someone knew they might be inheriting the land, the trees, and whatever money Nettie had stashed away and wanted to get it before it lost value."

Right on cue, Brenda Castoe wound her way through the tables toward the booth.

"I'll tell you what I learned about coin sellers when we get back to your place tonight," Joseph whispered.

"My turn to host?" I grinned over at her.

"Damn right," she said, smiling back. "I want to be there in the morning when you go looking for that bag of gold."

13

Brenda Castoe had not met Joseph in person and responded to the introduction with an interest and graciousness that convinced me she either had nothing to do with Nettie's murder or was the coolest killer I'd ever come across, not that I'd run into that many in my short tenure as sheriff. After the waitress took our orders, she and Joseph filled the time until our food was served talking about her work and the number of clients she had scattered throughout the hill country. "There are a number in the county," she told us, "and almost all are women." She glanced over at me with a wry smile.

"Older men who live by themselves don't seem to feel the need to carry emergency alerts. Of the fifteen I check on down your way, eleven are women. Well, ten, now that Nettie's gone."

"How would you describe your relationship with Nettie?" I interjected. Joseph yielded the lead, turning to her salad.

Brenda's face beamed. "Oh, we really enjoyed each other. She didn't seem to have any family and, with the exception of her minister who I think stopped by about once a month, she didn't have visitors. No neighbors close by, except for that good-for-nothing father and son who have the place behind her. She absolutely detested them. I always made sure I had a couple of hours to spend with her. Even then, I had to tear myself away. She was a very lonely woman."

"You mentioned the Greaves. The men down the holler. Did she ever say anything about having a run-in with them? Or any trouble?"

Brenda shook her head slowly, looking down at fish tacos

she was yet to touch. "No. In fact, I think she avoided them like the plague. When we talked about the valley being flooded, she once said she hoped it would happen when they'd drunk themselves into a stupor and just got covered over by it. Said it would be better for everyone."

"Did she say what she was planning to do? I think she only had eight to ten months to find another place."

"She'd talked to the people at The Oaks about moving in there."

Joseph gave me an inquiring look and I answered as much for her as for Brenda. "The assisted living center in town?"

"Yes. The last time I visited, she'd just been in to look at a one-bedroom unit and was complaining about how little space it would give her. But she seemed resigned to making the move."

Joseph laid down her fork and jumped back into the conversation. "Did she say how she was going to pay for the place? We've found that she wasn't registered with Social Security, didn't have Medicare or Medicaid, and had no bank account that we can find."

Brenda shrugged. "When I asked her about possible Medicare or insurance help with her alert plan, she said she had a regular source of income that would take care of it and paid me in cash for a year in advance. I had the impression she would prefer not to discuss the details, so I didn't ask."

Joseph cast me a glance that said, "You get to tell her the big news" and turned back to her salad.

"What would you say," I began, "if I told you Nettie has named you in her will as her sole beneficiary?"

Brenda's face tightened into a troubled frown and her hands dropped into her lap. She sat in silence for a few moments, then stammered, "Why, I wouldn't know *what* to say." The surprise struck me as completely genuine.

"That appears to be the case."

"Well, I'm completely flabbergasted. And I think the agency might be concerned. They are *very* clear with us that they don't want to ever hear that we might be taking advantage of a client."

"Do you think you took advantage of Nettie?"

The woman's eyes flashed. "Not in the least. I tried to be a friend. And she really had absolutely nothing to covet."

"Three hundred acres for which she will probably receive almost a million dollars in the buyout. Plus, the value of the timber."

Brenda's indignation caught fire. "I had no idea her property would have that kind of value. It was going to be turned into a lake that would bury an old, beat-up mobile home." She stared daggers at Joseph. "Are you two insinuating that I might have had something to do with Nettie's death?" She shifted her glare back at me. "I called you about being concerned something was wrong, in case you've forgotten."

I lifted a calming hand. "We aren't insinuating anything. We simply wanted to know if you were aware that you are named in her will as her sole heir. Apparently, the answer is no."

"I wasn't aware, and I am completely shocked."

"Hmm," I grunted. "Well, the will hasn't been filed yet. We saw it only because of a warrant. But I'm sure you'll be notified fairly soon. What would you do with that kind of money?" I saw no reason to mention the Confederate coins.

"I have no idea whatsoever." She slid from the booth, looked at both of us with what appeared to be genuine confusion, then down at the untouched tacos.

"One of you can take those with you. I don't think I can eat a thing. I need to go somewhere and think this all over."

Joseph handed her a card. "I do have one more question. The pathologist estimated that Nettie died two days before you called Sheriff Tate out to the house. Do you recall what you were doing on that Wednesday?"

Focus returned to Brenda Castoe's eyes. "And you aren't insinuating anything?" she said sharply. "That sounds like quite an insinuation."

"We're asking the same of everyone associated with the woman," Joseph answered evenly. "Do you recall?"

Brenda dug a small notebook out of her handbag. "I can tell you exactly." She flipped through the pages, looking for the date, then held it out to Joseph. "There. Those were my appointments and times. I was up around Willard all day. And you will note that I had an evening meeting of the Friends of the Library. I can copy these pages and send them to you if you like."

"I'd appreciate that. We'll probably be getting in touch with you again. In the meantime, if there's anything you think might be helpful or if you'd like to just talk, give me a call."

The woman cast us each a more resentful look, then turned and quickly left the restaurant.

I had only ordered a drink and reached over to take one of the fish tacos. "So . . . what do you make of that?"

Joseph pushed her salad aside and took the other taco. "Either stunned or an Academy Award performance," she answered.

As we drove to her apartment to pick up some creek clothes and get her car, she briefed me on what she had learned about gold and coin buyers in and around Springfield. Including pawn shops and jewelers who bought precious metals, she'd developed a list of twenty-four. During the morning, she had managed to visit seven.

"I started with the actual coin shops," she explained, propping a list on her knee. "I figured Nettie would know enough to realize the coins were worth more than the gold content and would get a better deal from a dealer than from a pawn shop. And from the fact she was living off the sales, I think we can assume she was getting a pretty decent price. Your library visit this morning suggests she knew the value of what she had. The first guy I talked to confirmed that a jeweler or pawn broker would call one of the people who knew old coins before making an offer on something like that. All of them were pretty certain none of the dollars had surfaced around town."

"Because . . . ?" I prompted.

"Well, like you said, these are pretty special coins. They didn't give me a price. In fact, two of them said they wouldn't even guess without seeing one. But all agreed that if one was circulating, it would have been big news in their tight little circle."

"Maybe she did just sell them for the value of the gold."

"I don't think so. When I asked one dealer, he said a person couldn't live long on the gold value in one or two. And even a pretty inexperienced pawn broker would know they had something pretty unusual and would try to get more information. There are a couple in Nixa we can check with on the way down, but I don't think the old girl sold them in the Springfield area."

"Had any seen them for sale recently?"

"One of the coin dealers said he saw an Indian Princess in mint condition advertised for auction on one of the trade websites. He thought the seller was a dealer in Mexico. In his mind, that raised question about the coin's authenticity."

"Yeah, it would," I agreed, but made a mental note to check out sales of 1861-Ds from south of the border.

14

That night with Mara Joseph curled up in the spare room down the hall was the most restless I'd had in a long time. She had followed me down in her own car. We made a couple of fruitless stops at pawnshops and jewelry stores in Nixa, then a more productive one to buy tomato sauce, ground beef, and a loaf of French bread at Family Market as we drove through town. Jerry winked at me across the meat counter when I picked up the hamburger, nodding knowingly at the state patrolwoman.

"Gotcha quite a new partner there, Tate. I talked to her yesterday and I approve."

"Working on the Suskey case," I defended.

"That's what she said. But you two look good together."

I glanced over to see if Joseph, who was scanning shelves in the bread aisle, was close enough to hear. "Better keep that comment on your side of the counter," I begged, knowing he wouldn't.

When we got to the house, Joseph tossed a salad while I made meatballs and mixed up a panful of my mother's favorite pasta and topping. Mara moved around the kitchen like she knew instinctively where everything would be. When we carried our plates and a bottle of wine out onto the deck, I was thinking I hadn't had such a perfect evening since losing Adeena.

The sun was low in the west end of the valley and the air was cool without being chilly. A heron strutted in the shallows of the creek below, and somewhere in the woods north of the house a pileated woodpecker drummed on a dying oak. I didn't want to talk business.

"So," I said, lifting a steaming helping of spaghetti onto her plate, "you got the thumbnail on my past last evening. Tell me about how a Jewish girl from University City ended up as a state patrol investigator?"

She shrugged as if there weren't much to tell. "College up at Truman State. Law school at Washington U. I did an internship with the FBI in Miami between my second and third years and was introduced to the human trafficking issues we face in this country. Everywhere, including our sheltered Midwestern state. So I decided to skip the practice of law and go into enforcement."

"But not with the Bureau?"

Her smile was the first sign of shyness I'd seen in Mara Joseph. "I guess I'm actually a bit of a homebody," she confessed. "I didn't want to be moving all around the country and thought I could do the most good close to home."

"I think I know the feeling," I agreed, and we spent the rest of the evening admiring the heron and watching barn swallows begin to swoop and glide over the creek.

During the night I made two trips into the kitchen for a drink. Maybe she'd hear me and come out—give me just enough encouragement to feel like I wasn't being too presumptive if I pulled her close and kissed her. But even with a little extra noise filling a glass, nothing stirred in the spare room. And today's climate is no time for a man to be initiating anything without some pretty obvious encouragement.

I was up and had coffee steaming and omelets on the stove when she came into the kitchen. She'd dressed in the clothes I'd suggested for the morning: a pair of old shorts, T-shirt, and tennis shoes with a decent tread. The outfit did nothing to dampen my admiration. A body that had looked compact under a pair of jeans and a state investigator's shirt now showed itself to be trim and finely muscled. I couldn't resist a comment.

"You look like you must be a runner."

Her laugh was bright enough to show appreciation. "I hate running. But I'm a stationary bike fanatic. The gym I go to has the kind with the screen that lets me ride through the French countryside or up over the Alps if I feel up to it." She looked at me critically. "You don't look like you dressed for the wading you told me to be ready for."

I'd slipped on a loose pair of sweatpants and a St. Louis Cardinals T-shirt. "It'll take me about two seconds to change. If we eat out on the deck, you might want some repellant on your legs."

"I'm fine inside this morning. The omelets smell great. Have you had coffee yet?"

"Waiting for you." That earned another appreciative smile.

She helped me clear and wash as if each of us had well-rehearsed assignments, then put dishes away while I stepped into the bedroom and changed into an old knee-length pair of black and yellow swim trunks and a T-shirt from the town's last charity 5-K for the high school softball team. Joseph was standing at the door when I came out with keys to the Explorer and a couple of old beach towels. She gave me her own once-over. "It looks to me like you're the runner."

"Not really. I heat the place with wood in the winter and spend a lot of time cutting and splitting. And I like to jog the back trails around here in the morning."

"It seems to work." She held out the keys.

We parked again at the end of Nettie's path where yellow crime scene tape still stretched across the front of the trailer. I led Joseph around back and along a faint trail that crossed an acre of meadow, then cut through the woods toward the bend where the creek swept against the bluff.

"Watch for poison ivy," I cautioned. "You look like you escaped the last round, but with shorts on, you won't be so lucky." I pointed at a patch of the low, three-leafed plant and guided her around it.

The path exited the woods where the creek first brushed the rocky cliffside. Between us and the place I thought Nettie's letter had described, a deep pool had been swept from the gravel bed. This late in the year, the water ran slow and clear as poured glass.

"Can you swim?" I asked, realizing it was a little late to be raising the question.

Joseph moved to the edge of the bank. "I can. But how do we pull ourselves up out of the water to get up that bluff? And by the way, this looks a whole lot more like a river than a creek."

I chuckled. "Everything down here's a creek, no matter how wide. And we don't pull ourselves up the bank. When I asked about swimming, I was just thinking about what would happen if you slipped back into that pool. It'll be head-deep on you."

"Slip from where?" She glanced across at the thirty-foot rock face that rose directly out of the stream.

"The water's only knee-deep here. I used to float this creek six or eight times a year when I was a kid. This part hasn't changed much. Over there along the bluff, there's a narrow rock shelf about two feet under the water. We'll wade across here, then slide along that shelf." I pointed at another ledge chest-high above the water and fifty feet to our left. "I think that must be the place Ezra Suskey's letter talked about."

Joseph look down along our side of the pool. "It would be good if we could get across from it and take a better look."

The clay bank on our side rose steeply into a thick tangle of brambles. "I don't think you want to go through that stuff. It will scratch you to pieces and cover you with chiggers. Just follow me across and we'll edge our way over to the ledge. It's going to be slippery as hell from algae, but if we slide our feet along, I think we can scrape a foothold as we go."

She shrugged. "You're the creek guide. Lead on."

Algae had also turned the pebbled bottom into a skateland, and we slipped and splashed our way through leg-numbing water to where the ledge left the gravel as the bottom plunged into the deeper pool. I pressed against the rock face and scraped my left sole along the surface, clearing a foothold as I went. Joseph clung tightly to the sleeve of my T-shirt, gripping what she could of the rock with her other hand. As we reached Ezra Suskey's ledge, the narrow shelf met me right at chest-high and provided extra leverage as I steadied myself just past the flat cover stone the letter had described. Joseph's eyes fell midway up the slab.

"Can you brace yourself well enough to slide that thing?" she asked. "It looks heavy."

I splashed water up onto the ledge and gripped the lip of the ledge with my left hand. "I'll pull and you push," I suggested. "On three."

On the three-count, we both heaved against the rock plate, moving it a good foot along the ledge.

"How did that little lady move this thing?" Joseph wondered aloud. "It must weight forty or fifty pounds."

I scraped again at the ledge under our feet. "My guess is that she came when the creek's low enough that this shelf we're on is above water and dry. If we could brace our feet, this wouldn't be so hard. Now, once more." The second surge slid the rock far enough that the crevice behind it was partially exposed. I was able to get my right hand up against the edge of the slab and force it another six inches. Joseph gazed into the notch.

"I see it," she whispered, as if other ears might be listening. "It looks like a canvas bag, about as big as a lunch sack."

"Can you reach it?"

"Not without letting go of what's holding me up here. Namely, you."

"I'll give it try." Tightening my grip on the rock shelf, I

released the edge of the stone cover and thrust my right hand into the opening. The cloth of the bag was surprisingly firm. I wrapped a hand around the neck and pulled outward. The motion shifted Joseph's grip on my arm and I felt her let go, grasp wildly for another handhold, and tumble backward toward the pool. Before I could release the sack to reach for her, the stone where her head had been shattered into fragments, followed instantly by the sharp crack of a rifle report.

With bag in hand, I threw myself backward after Joseph into the pool, feeling the sting of shrapnel against the side of my head and neck. Twisting onto my stomach as I entered the water, I thrust my feet downward, searching for the bottom as I peered through the churning water for my partner.

My feet told me the pool was shallow enough that if I stood, my face would be above water. The shot, I was certain, had come from the ridgeline on the other side of the hollow. The shooter would have been able to see us on the ledge, but not down on the surface where the overgrown bank gave us cover. A hand grabbed my shirt, pulling me under.

I pushed into the gravel with my feet and stood, chin barely clearing the surface. Joseph thrashed beside me, trying to tread water and haul me toward the bank. I wrapped my free arm about her waist and pulled her against me, whispering into her ear.

"I'm standing. Just relax. I'll get us against the bank. Were you hit?"

"Was I hit?" she gasped. "By what? I just fell when your arm pulled back."

"Someone shot at us just as you tumbled backward. From up behind us. We should be out of sight now, but they may come down here after us." I dragged us downstream until the bank lowered and I could push her out beneath a tangle of honeysuckle and scramble after her. I pulled her tightly against my side, tucked the canvas bag against my other hip, and waited.

ALLEN KENT

15

If a car had driven away on the ridge road, it had happened
while we were thrashing about in the pool. I hadn't heard
engine or tire noise. We remained immobile, pressed flat
beneath a screen of twisted leaves and stems. Through a break
in the cover, I could see two red squirrels chasing each other up
the checkered trunk of a persimmon. Somewhere overhead, a
pileated chattered, announcing an all-clear.

I pulled a finger up across Joseph's lips, whispered "stay" in
the ear that was inches from my own lips, and tucked the sack
in against her stomach. As I eased backward, my neck sliding
along her hip and legs, a crimson streak painted her shorts and
exposed skin. The sting above my ear seeped blood where a
fragment of rock had cut into my hairline. Back in the stream, I
stripped off my shirt, ripped it into wide strips, and tied a tight
band over the larger cut on my head. Sitting back against the
current, I let it drift me downstream.

At the first break in the brush, I pulled myself onto the bank
and scrambled back into the woods at a low crouch, skirting the
pasture and moving quietly through the thick stand of walnuts
until within sight of Nettie's trailer. If the attacker was waiting,
he would be watching the patrol car from the hill opposite the
creek. Slipping around the house on the stream side, I crouched
at the corner, scanned the ridge for movement and, seeing
none, zig-zagged to the back of the Explorer. The ridge
remained quiet.

My weapon of choice is a Sig P320, the civilian version of
the military's M17. I'd stashed mine in a small gun safe
secured behind the rear seat of the Ford when we went to the

creek. Cracking the rear hatch, I slithered in and retrieved the weapon, then tumbled over the seat to the radio.

"Grace, can you pick up?"

She answered immediately. "Yeah, Tate. Where've you been? I've been trying to call you."

"Go to secure," I said, directing her to a frequency away from the standard department setting. Monitoring police calls is popular entertainment around the county and this conversation needed to be private. I switched to the safe frequency and waited for her "I'm on. What's up?"

"I'm with Officer Joseph out at Nettie's. We were just fired on from the ridge. Can you run out here and cruise the road to see if anyone's camped up there? The shot came from about a quarter mile this side of Darnell's place."

"On my way. Are you alright?"

"Yeh. Missed us by a fraction of an inch."

"Where are you now?"

"I'm at the cruiser in front of Nettie's. Joseph's hunkered down back along the bend in the creek. If we're not at the car, come look for us there."

"Be there in fifteen," she said.

I slipped out of the Explorer and twisted back through the trees to the edge of the stream where we had first entered the water. The shot had smashed into the rock face just to the right of the crevice, leaving a crater the size of a dinner plate. Any bullet fragments had tumbled back into the pool.

"You okay, Joseph?" I called down the bank.

"I'm here. Did you find anything?" She began to back out of the honeysuckle clump.

"Wait. I'll come get the bag. It will take you right to the bottom. Float downstream and you'll see a place to climb out. Skirt back around here and take my weapon while I get the coins."

She slid backward until half in the water, perched the canvas sack on the bank, then dropped into the current. I waited until she could circle around to cover me, then waded the sack out of the stream. As we made our way back to the squad car, she swept the woods around us with the Sig. From the end of Nettie's trailer, we sprinted one at a time to the rear of the Ford, squatted together against the bumper, then swung the hatch open. I plopped the wet bag onto the rubber matting of the rear compartment. Up on the ridge road, Grace ran her siren through a couple of cycles to clear the area.

"Want to take a look before company arrives?" Joseph wondered.

"Damn right—after all that." The top of the bag was cinched with a tightly knotted leather thong that broke away as I tugged at it. I spilled the contents onto the mat.

"*Oy vey*," Joseph exclaimed under her breath. "There's a fortune here. And they all look in mint condition." She glanced past me as Grace turned her car down the hill. "You ready to show these to your deputy?"

I quickly counted seventeen bright Indian Princess dollars. "Not 'til we know more." I scooped them back into the sack, spun open the gun safe, and thrust them into the back, followed by the Sig. Grace swung her cruiser up beside us and climbed out.

"I thought you said you didn't get hit," she exclaimed, looking us over critically and settling on my stained headband.

I fingered the blood-soaked strip. "A couple of pieces of rock grazed me. I don't think it's too bad."

"You better get in and have that checked." She shifted her gaze to Joseph with what I read as unveiled disapproval. "Have you two been getting in a little creek time?"

I looked down at my bare chest, then over at the shirt and shorts that clung to Joseph like cellophane. "We dove in when the shot passed over our heads," I lied. "It seemed like the best cover."

"You were standing by the creek when the shot came? Dressed like that?"

"We were trying to get a measure of how much timber Nettie has that's still uncut. I thought we might need to do a little wading. If the Greaves weren't in jail, I'd of guessed it was one of them who shot at us."

Grace continued to measure the wet inspector. "I got bad news for you, Tate. Judge Werner said we either had to charge Verl or let him go. I had to turn him loose this morning."

"We couldn't hold him on the video I sent of the cut trees?"

"He said they had permission. There's really no one who can refute that."

"*Shit.*" The word slipped out before I could stifle it. "Excuse the French," I said to Joseph, then turned back to Grace. "Is that what you were trying to call me about?"

"That, and something even more complicating. I had an office visit this morning. Do you know anything about a Galen Suskey?"

The name tinkled a very small chime back in the recesses of my memory. An overheard conversation about Nettie at dinner when I was a kid visiting my uncle's place on the ridge. Uncle Jack had asked Mother, "You know what happened to Nettie's no-good brother Galen?" Mother had shrugged and said, "He was a few years younger than Nettie. I remember our Dad telling us once that Galen was a trouble-maker and dropped out of school at about fifteen. Took off, and hasn't been seen since."

"Yeah. I vaguely remember mention of him, Grace," I said. "Why?"

"He came in this morning. Wants to talk to you. I told him to come back this afternoon after 2:00, thinking you might decide to come into work."

I shot her a disapproving frown, knowing as I did that she was right. I hadn't been checking in like I should have been.

"So, he decided to show up all of a sudden after all these years. Where's he been, and how did he learn about Nettie's death?"

Grace returned my frown with a tight-lipped smirk. "We didn't chat much. He wanted to talk to 'the real sheriff.' So I told him to come back, and I'd try to find out what the real sheriff was up to." She cast Joseph another sidelong glance. "When you get yourself changed, you might both want to meet with him. He'll be impressed to have a *real* state investigator, too. But I should warn you. This old guy is a real piece of work."

16

Joseph drove as we climbed back up the drive out of the holler with Grace trailing close behind. We turned left toward my place. Grace went right to stop by Darnell's studio to see if he'd seen anyone pass on the ridge road. And the shot had been close enough that he might have heard it.

Joseph was silent until the other squad car disappeared behind us, then said, "As soon as we get changed, I need to run you by the clinic to get your head checked. Then we'd better get those coins locked away somewhere safe."

Without the distraction of the sprint from the creek and the bag of gold dollars, the cut over my ear was beginning to throb. I had to focus for a minute to sort through what she'd said.

"The department's got what used to be the vault of the bank," I said finally, addressing what seemed most important. "We use it as our evidence locker. Probably more secure than anything most departments have. Deputy D'Amico keeps an eye on it. But once I put the coins in one of the old safe deposit boxes and label it 'restricted access,' he won't bother it without checking with me. I need to get Ezra Suskey's letter in with it. That's still at the house."

"They'll be alright in the gun safe until we get your head looked at. That needs to be first."

I saw no reason to argue, and the cut was starting to ache like the dickens.

We drove for another couple of minutes in silence then, out of the blue, she said, "I think your Girl Friday has some issues."

I'd been thinking about the shot from the ridge that had

almost killed the inspector, and her comment made no sense at all.

"My Girl Friday? What are you talking about?"

"Your chief deputy. She's got some issues?"

"Grace? What kind of issues?"

"With me. Couldn't you see it?"

I shrugged. "She looked a little annoyed, but I think that was from being dragged out to check on a shooter."

"No. She doesn't like you working with me."

I fingered the cut that was beginning to swell. "Ah, don't be crazy. Why would Grace care if I was working with you?"

Joseph glanced over with a thin smile. "I don't think she likes another woman getting your attention."

I sniffed. "I thought I told you, she has a steady boyfriend."

"Maybe that's because she doesn't see you as being in play."

I started to untie the bandage to have a look at the cut in the visor mirror.

"Leave that thing in place," she ordered. "It's stopped bleeding. You'll just open it up again."

I re-cinched the knot and sat back restlessly. I didn't like where Joseph's conversation was taking us.

"Are you in play?" she pressed.

"I'm not sure what you mean by that."

"Have you been out with anyone since you lost Adeena?"

"What's that got to do with you or Grace?"

"I'll take that to be a 'no.'" She wasn't going to let the subject drop.

"Have you ever lost someone you truly loved?" I asked.

"My father."

"No. I mean passionately loved. Had given your whole heart and soul to."

"No. I can't say that I've ever cared for anyone like that." We had turned down my drive and were parked in front of the house.

"It's not something you get over easily. And not a kind of pain you want to set yourself up for again."

Joseph turned off the ignition and sat frowning into her lap. "I can understand that. And I imagine Grace Torres does too. But that doesn't mean she doesn't have some pretty strong feelings for you."

I shook off the suggestion. "And you think you could tell that from the five minutes we spent in front of Nettie's."

She continued to stare downward. "A woman can tell. Especially when she's been wondering some of the same things herself."

Now, I know I'm a guy and can be pretty clueless about some of this stuff. But I hadn't seen this coming. Admittedly, it hadn't escaped me that Joseph was very easy on the eyes, especially in that clinging shirt and pair of shorts. And I'd had my little fantasy the night before about bumping into each other in the kitchen and ending up in the same bedroom. But this was starting to get too close to serious relationship talk. And it seemed all the stranger with me sitting next to this woman wearing only a pair of damp shorts, with my shirt tied around my head.

"I think you misread Grace," I said lamely. "She's never given me any indication I was anything to her but her boss. And as for being 'in play?' I've never really thought about it since Adeena died."

Joseph smiled faintly, shifted her gaze out the window, then sucked in a deep breath and straightened in the seat. "Just something I noticed," she said, and opened the car door. "We'd better get some dry clothes on and get your head looked at. Then to your office to get the coins locked away and meet with this Galen Suskey. And if you're feeling up to it, I think I'd like to go looking for Verl Greaves."

17

Galen Suskey was a male version of his sister, a squat, gnome of a man with shaggy gray hair that looked like it hadn't been washed in the last month and two weeks of stubble on his craggy face. His rumpled clothes hung like a dust cover over an old sofa. He hunched into the office, looked around uneasily for a chair he thought might accommodate his stumpy legs, and decided to stand.

I had been kicked back behind the desk, talking to Grace about where we might launch a search for Verl Greaves. Joseph had decided she would leave Galen Suskey to me and had driven back to Springfield to catch up on her own office work. Grace was beside the window in a wooden armchair, eliminating the choice that might have appealed most to the man. We both stood when he came in. I pulled one of two straight-backed wooden chairs over in front of the desk and he hoisted himself reluctantly up onto it, feet dangling a few inches from the floor.

I nodded toward Grace. "You met Officer Torres when you came in this morning. I'm Sheriff Tate."

He ignored Grace. "Yeah. I remember you Tates. Lived up on the ridge. You must be one of Ed's grandsons. Jack's kid or Marvin's?"

"Marvin's."

Suskey nodded his shaggy head. "I heard he got killed years back cutting timber."

"Yes, he did. And I'm very sorry about the loss of your sister. I assume that's what you wanted to meet with me about."

His jaw bounced in a continuous chew of loose-fitting denture. "Yeah. What happened to her?" he asked, the teeth clicking loudly on the "to."

"As I'm sure you've been told, she was murdered. It appears someone smothered her."

The man's sour expression didn't change. "Robbed her place?"

I leaned back in my chair. "You must have heard about this, to be back in town asking. Who contacted you about it?" As far as I knew, no one had spoken publicly about Nettie's house having been burglarized.

"I still know people around. They let me know what's going on."

"Told you she'd been killed and that it might have been a burglary?"

He cocked his head, his jaw tightening around the dentures. "Might 'a told me that. I was just wondering what you think happened."

"That's all still under investigation. If someone did try to rob the place, what would they have been after? Nettie didn't seem to have much of anything."

"Beats the hell out of me. I haven't seen her in over fifty years. But it ain't right. Someone killing her like that."

"And where have you been, this past fifty years, Mr. Suskey?"

He nodded toward the door. "Been livin' over in Oklahoma. Worked the oil fields until I was too old and stoved up to handle the pipe. Since then, just been hangin' on to life."

"Where would that be in Oklahoma? You have an address?" Grace pulled a pad from a hip pocket, causing Suskey to swivel toward her on the chair.

"What do you need an address for? I'm the one here asking about Nettie."

"We're following up on everyone who might have had any connection with her," I said.

The little man swung back toward me. "I just told you, I ain't seen Nettie since I left this hellhole of a town fifty years ago."

"Then giving us an address shouldn't be a problem," Grace said from the window.

Suskey shrugged. "I was workin' in Bartlesville. Left there when I stopped and have a place over in Nowata."

"Address?" Grace repeated. He gave her what sounded like an apartment number on West Wettack Avenue.

"So, you've come back to make arrangements for Nettie?"

His face crumpled into a puzzled frown. "I thought she'd be buried or cremated or something by now."

I glanced over at Grace who arched a surprised brow.

"There had to be some forensic work because of the murder. She's still up in Springfield at the morgue."

Galen Suskey squirmed uncomfortably on the unforgiving chair. "I imagine she'll have some friends and church people who will take care of putting her away," he muttered. "We didn't even know each other."

Grace had been sitting back, pad and pen on her lap, and leaned forward with elbows on her knees. "Then, what are you here for, Mr. Suskey?" she asked acidly.

Without feet on the floor to brace him, the squat little body had to turn entirely at the waist to face her, a challenging feat for such a thick torso. He groaned a little as he turned, throwing his hips enough to be able to look at the deputy.

"I'm here for the farm," he said bluntly. "Nobody really never gave it to her. She just kept living there when Ma and Pa died. I figure it's as much mine as hers."

Grace held on to our side of the conversation. "That would all have to be decided by probate," she said coolly. "We haven't come across any documents that show your parents left the farm to Nettie, but that will all have to be checked out. The judge will assign someone to determine what happens to the estate."

"What the hell is probate?" Suskey snarled. "That's my farm, and ain't nobody going to tell me it ain't."

Grace's dark eyes cooled to icy coals. "I'm telling you it ain't. At least, not yet. And you need to stay away from the place until Nettie's will gets through probate, which means the court decides what happens to her property."

The little man turned back toward me. "Who's the sheriff around here anyway? You, or this pollo?"

I bolted up out of the chair and leaned toward him over the desk. "Alright, Mr. Suskey. We won't have any of that kind of talk in this office. One more comment like that and you're out of here. And Officer Torres is exactly right. You have no claim on that property until the judge says you do."

"Ain't just *her* property," the gnome spit back. "That's family property. My grandpappy settled there, and it's been in the family ever since. And what's this about a will? She forget she had a brother?"

"Seems most everyone forgot she had a brother," I offered, lowering myself slowly back into the chair. "And Grace is also right that this is a discussion between you and the court. You might be smart to go visit with Able Pendergraft. Get some legal help."

"Shit. I can't afford no lawyer. And Able Pendergraft? Whose kid is he? We got a Tate for Sheriff, and some Pendergraft kid's the lawyer?"

"Able's not exactly a kid," Grace snorted. "Must be in his upper sixties."

Galen Suskey kept his eyes on me. He'd had enough turning in the chair. "I ain't getting no lawyer. But I need to get claim to my farm before they flood the damn thing."

It was my turn to arch a brow. "So you're aware the holler's going to be covered by the new reservoir. When did you learn this?"

Suskey slouched forward, glaring across the desk. "Like I said, I know people here. They tell me things."

"Hmm," I muttered. "How long have you known about the water project?"

"You mean the flooding? From about the time they said they was going to do it."

"But you didn't decide to come check on the place until you

learned that Nettie was dead."

"No reason to while she was living."

"But I understood you to say that you believed the property to be as much yours as hers. Weren't you concerned about what might happen to it?"

"Hell, yes! But I . . . I. . . " He looked at his knees, stammering into the floor. "I figured if Nettie got paid for it, half of that would be mine too. Easier to split the money than the farm. I'd come after it then."

I completed the thought for him. "When Nettie died, you mean?"

"*No*," he barked. "I'd come claim my half when I knew she'd been paid off."

"So you were going to wait until you heard from this friend that the property had sold. Is that the way it was going to work?"

He kept his eyes lowered. "Yup. That's what I was plannin'."

"And what are you thinking to do now?" Grace asked.

He shrugged. "Who do I see about getting this probate?"

I pushed out of the chair, inviting Grace to stand with me. "That would be Judge Werner. You'll find his office over in the courthouse."

Suskey tilted forward off of the chair. "Ain't nobody going to steal my property from me," he muttered, and stalked out of the office.

Grace walked over to join me as I circled the desk, both of us arriving too late to get the door for our visitor. We stood in silence until we heard the outer door bang shut.

"What a poor excuse for a human being," she murmured. "The man isn't even concerned about burying his own sister."

I grunted in agreement. "The thing that surprised me was that he wasn't at all concerned about what thieves might have been after. I'd think he'd be wondering what Nettie had that anyone would come kill her for."

"I've wondered that myself," Grace said. "The old lady didn't seem to have two dimes to rub together. She had all that property. But there was no reason to tear up her house for that."

For the first time since the whole murder thing began, I realized that the person who had been my major supporter and partner up to Joseph's arrival was being shut out of some of the most important information related to this case. Was it really because I thought we needed to keep the gold out of the equation until Joseph and I knew more? And that I didn't trust Grace to be discreet? No. If I was honest, I just liked having a little secret that I shared with Joseph. Pretty junior high, now that I thought about it. Pretty unfair to my Number Two, and definitely second-class law enforcement.

"Come with me," I said, taking her by the elbow. "There's something you need to know about that I should have shown you this morning." I walked her back through the office toward the old vault. "And when I've shown you this, I need to have you find out everything you can about where Galen Suskey's been the last few weeks and who's been feeding him information."

18

Joseph came to the office the next morning just after 9:00, refused one of the breakfast burritos Marti had ordered in from LeeAnn's Café and Bakery on the south side of the square, and sat nervously while I passed out the morning's assignments. Grace was still looking for Galen Suskey's connection in Crayton. An abandoned pickup had been left half-submerged in a pond up off Highway MM and needed Deputy Ritter's attention. Rocky D'Amico was going to make his rounds of shops in town, doing a little PR work and seeing if there was any useful speculation about who might have killed Nettie. Joseph and I went looking for Verl Greaves.

This time we didn't stop on the Greaves' drive to shout down the hill, just barreled full-tilt up to the front of their metal building, threw our doors open, and crouched behind them, weapons drawn. The pit bulls launched themselves against the wire of their pen, black lips curled and foaming.

"Verl, you in there?" I shouted over the snarling dogs. No answer. "Verl, we're coming in. If you're armed, lay down your weapon 'cause I'm not going to warn you again. If your hands aren't in plain sight when we come in, we'll shoot." Not a sound.

Joseph sprinted from behind her door to a stack of fifty-gallon drums that stood in knee-high weeds beside the engine hoist. With her in place, I zig-zagged to the building's front corner, flattened against the side, and made my way to the edge of the smaller door. Joseph followed, pressing against the metal on the other side of the frame. A hand-painted sign beside the door warned in black, block letters, "KEEP OUT.

TRESPASERS WILL BE SHOT." I reached across and tried the handle. It moved freely.

"Verl, we're coming in!" I gave him a silent three-count to reply, threw the door open, and flipped back out of the way. Joseph looked across at me, gestured that she would go in low, and mouthed, "On three." On the third bob of her head, we swung into the room, Joseph in a low squat, me sliding across the doorway with weapon extended.

The interior was one large room, divided only by piles of junk and garbage. One front corner, the floor strewn with discarded food packaging and empty cans, served as a kitchen. A propane stove was vented through the metal sidewall and a single length of insulated PVC pipe brought cold water in from an outside well. The plastic sink below it overflowed with crusted dishes. The whole interior smelled of spoiled food.

The front space opposite the kitchen was a jumble of sofas and chairs, some pushed into the background and stacked on top of each other as they split a seam or cracked across a vinyl cushion. The more serviceable seats formed a crude circle, grouped around a dozen coffee and end tables of every shape and height, each heaped with worn tools, machine parts, grease-covered clothing, and more torn food wrappers. A channel no wider than the men's shoulders disappeared into the back between the nearest sofa and the mounds of kitchen rubble, cast in dim light by the open door.

"Verl?" I shouted into the dark interior, the sound instantly sucked up by the hoarder's squalor. I started toward the gap, stopped short by a shout from Joseph.

"*Wait.*" She stepped forward, drawing an LED penlight from a pocket. She flashed it at the floor a yard into the passage. A fine strand of wire crossed the gap six inches above the bare concrete slab. I eased carefully over it, then knelt and tracked it beneath a sofa, up the back of a pick handle, and into a stack of slatted crates. Joseph handed her light over the wire and I peered between slats into the barrel of a 12-gauge shotgun.

"We're out of here," I whispered. "There may be a bunch of these hidden around. We need a team that can take this place apart from front to back." I stepped back over the wire and followed Joseph out into the sunlight. She nodded back at the misspelled sign beside the entrance and frowned cynically. "Can't say we weren't warned."

"Do you think that covers them? If one of us got blown away?" I was feeling like a novice again.

Joseph shook her head. "Booby traps are illegal, even in your own house. We have a warrant. So the discovery is legal. We now have good grounds for arresting and holding Verl."

"Do you think he was back in that heap somewhere?"

"No truck. And the dog's bowls are empty. We probably should call Animal Rescue and get them picked up."

The cell buzzed in my pocket. It was Grace. I listened, trying to shut out the earlier conversation with Joseph, thanked her, and hit the end button.

"Galen Suskey moved out of his rental in Nowata three weeks ago," I repeated to Joseph. "The landlady didn't have any idea where he went."

"So, three missing weeks until he shows up here."

"Grace is checking on that."

"And on you," she grinned. "That bit of news could have waited until she saw you later today."

"Down here, we keep each other informed."

Joseph raised a skeptical brow and slipped into the passenger side of the cruiser. "So—what's next?"

"Let's call Animal Rescue and get some of your state people down here to check this place out for more boobytraps—and put out an APB for Verl."

"If the traps didn't injure anyone, I'm not certain we have grounds for charges."

"Maybe the shot that was taken at us. But we can at least try to find out where he went when they released him from jail. And I want to walk a stretch of the ridge road where the shot came from. Darnell said he didn't hear the shot or anyone go by, but he was working on painting you into that hospital scene. He wouldn't have noticed a dozer crashing through his studio. If we're lucky, we'll find a casing for a Marlin 336."

I'd developed a theory about the shooting within minutes of Grace telling me Verl Greaves had been released. The way I saw it, he had passed the lane down to Nettie's on his way back to his rathole, seen the squad car parked in front, then continued to look down into the holler as he'd driven along the ridgeline. Somewhere in a break in the trees, he'd seen the two of us edging our way along the rock shelf, stopped his pickup, and taken the shot at Joseph.

"He picked you," I guessed as we drove slowly along the same stretch of road, looking for breaks in the trees, "because you were the one who shot LJ. If we hadn't fallen back into the creek, I think he would have tried for both of us."

We stopped at one of only two places we'd found where there was a good sightline to the bend in the stream.

"It would have taken a pretty good shot from here," Joseph muttered as we climbed from the cruiser and peered down over the edge of the pavement.

"His rifle is scoped," I reminded her, "and he may have just propped it in the open window of the pickup where he could keep it nice and steady."

"In which case, a casing may have ejected into the truck."

"May have. Depends on how he braced the thing in the window. Then again, he might have climbed out. He'd have been looking for us through the passenger window."

We split up and walked the pavement in both directions looking for a spent cartridge, then eased down into the grassy verge, repeating the sweep until low enough we could no longer see the creek below.

"Nothing on my side," Joseph called as she scrambled back up to the blacktop.

I raised my hands to show I'd had as little success. "Let's walk back down to that other break and see if we have better luck."

Fifty yards farther along the ridge, a narrower gap between oaks showed little more than the ten-foot stretch of ledge that had held the hidden coins. It was possible, I figured, that Verl had seen us through the first gap, slowed until he caught a glimpse through the second opening, and stopped to fire the shot from there. The tight break provided only one shooting position where thick lespedeza, our state highway department's contribution to invasive flora, clogged the shoulder. Joseph dove in, parting the knee-high brush a square foot at a time. I moved five steps to her left and followed suit. She was two minutes into her search when she struck pay dirt.

"Got it," she called, parting the brush with both hands. She broke a twig from a dry patch of the shrub, reached into the clump, and fished out a brass casing with the stick.

"Thirty-thirty?"

She turned it to look at the head stamp. "Yup. Winchester. Careless of him to leave it."

I scrambled back up through the brush, pulling a plastic evidence bag from a pocket. "If he didn't see where it went, he probably didn't want to risk hunting around for it in case somebody came by."

"Now," Joseph said, climbing up after me, "we just need a rifle to match it to or a good set of prints."

"I'm guessing there might be prints." I held the bag open and she dropped the empty cartridge into it. "Verl would have been given the Marlin when he was released from jail. The guy probably leaves it loaded in his truck and when he saw us, just stopped and took the shot. No planning, so no thought about prints on the rounds. Plus, I suspect the Greaves do their own reloading. When we get back into that place of theirs with some help, we might find casings Verl's already fired. If we can get a match, we're in business even without prints."

Joseph nodded. "It may be time to split up. I'll report back to my office and see if I can get some help with the house search. What's next on your list?"

I didn't need to consider the question. It had been eating at me since we left Springfield. "Mexico," I said. "I want to find out who's been selling Confederate gold in Mexico and where they got it."

19

Marti looked up expectantly when I pushed through the office door, then quickly back down at whatever she was typing. Not a warm "welcome back." Grace hunched forward at her desk, her cell squeezed between chin and shoulder, one hand scribbling notes while the other sorted through a loose stack of papers.

"I'll be out as soon as I can, Jim," she said patiently into the phone. "I've got the description of the trailer and the license number, though I'd guess whoever took it will have swapped the plates. I'll call the Arkansas patrol and the sheriffs' departments in the counties south of the line. They've been running these trailers down there and repainting them. Maybe we can catch it while it still has Bowman Cattle Company on the side."

She listened for a moment, then said, "Good. I'll tell them it's also etched into the underside of the tongue. Smart thing to do."

I skirted her desk, not escaping an icy stare.

"Be right back with you, Jim," she said evenly and swiped the phone from her chin with the notetaking hand.

"Good of you to stop in." She took a quick glance at the Fitbit that served as her watch. "Must have been able to do a little more investigating this afternoon."

I tried to ignore the sarcasm but felt it tighten the muscles along my jaw. "We made another stop at the Greaves place," I said too defensively. "Verl's gone, and we found the place boobytrapped. Officer Joseph's gone back up to Springfield to get some help sweeping the building. And . . ." I pulled the bag with the cartridge out of my pocket. ". . . we found a spent casing up on the ridge road. Thirty-thirty caliber."

"Nice work," she said coolly. "Fortunately, crime in the county has come to a complete standstill while you've been playing detective, except . . ." She glanced down at the page of notes that had been occupying her writing hand. ". . .someone just stole Jim Bowman's stock trailer. The big one he keeps chained beside the barn out on his south section. And Maria Hernandez called to complain that her husband was beating her up again. And . . . let me see . . . the school district called to report two children with bruises they think need to be investigated. And the Ridenours think someone may be cooking meth in an old shack at the back of their place. . . Shall I go on?"

"And Nettie Suskey got murdered in our county," I snapped back at her. "That hasn't happened while I've been in this job."

"But something like that will happen again. And you can't just stop doing everything else when it does. There are only two of us here in the office, and that's what the state police and your little investigator friend are out there for."

"It's our jurisdiction. They're just supposed to be additional resources."

"As much resource as we need to allow us to get other work done," Grace argued.

I knew she was right. I'd become obsessed with Nettie's murder and pretty enthralled with the company of Mara Joseph.

"You're right," I admitted. "I need to balance this out. I'll get a notice out about Bowman's trailer and run out to see him. I can check the shack out there behind Ridenour's place on my way back. Why don't you follow up on the kids and stop to talk to Maria? You know she'll have changed her mind about pressing charges by the time you get there. She always does."

"Fair enough. Is the inspector coming back with her people this evening?"

I shrugged what I hoped would look like a lack of real interest. "I don't know. She'll call when she has a team together."

Grace grunted a soft *humpf*. "One of us probably should be there when they go through the house."

"One of us should," I agreed.

She rose from her chair, pushed her weapon further back on her hip, and headed for the door. "We'll see who's available," she called back and didn't wait for a reply. Marti cast me another dark look, then buried herself again in her typing.

I tapped my computer to life and opened the browser. When the search box opened, I entered "1861-D dollar coin Mexico."

The top item on the list was Mazatlán Numismatics. A brief description said that the dealer in rare coins from across the Americas was again able to offer a rare, authenticated 1861-D gold dollar, minted by the Confederate States of the United States during the nation's Civil War. This was, the posting explained, the fifth such mint-perfect example of the very rare coin the dealer had acquired in as many years, but may be the last. The coin would be auctioned via a live tele-auction on November 30th.

I scanned to the bottom for the address. 1171 Angel Flores Pte., Mazatlán, Mexico. Five coins in five years. Just about the schedule Nettie would have followed to maintain her livelihood after she left the school cafeteria. And something to think about as I drove out to talk to Jim Bowman.

Joseph called at 9:45 as I was trying to decide whether to read myself to sleep with the newest Jacob Stone novel I was having trouble getting into or listen to a DVD of conversational Arabic to keep my language skills from rusting away. Late afternoon had been uneventful. Marti had called before I reached the Bowman place to let me know an observant Arkansas state patrolman had pulled over a stock trailer that met our description and appeared to have fresh spray paint on the side. Bowman Cattle Company was etched on the underside of the hitch tongue. Jim could drive down and claim his property in Harrison. When I reached Bowman's with the news, I looked like a hero, but I hadn't done squat.

The reported meth kitchen at the back of the Ridenour farm had moved, a spent butane cannister and a few aluminum pans left scattered about the old shed. If we'd run a drug-sniffing dog through the place, he'd have gone ballistic. But something had tipped off the cookers, and they had moved on to their next abandoned building. No victory for me there, but no messy drug raid either.

"We'll be down tomorrow," Joseph said when I answered. "Should get there about 10:15. Do you want me to call your cell when we get close?"

"Call the office," I suggested. "If Grace is free, I might have her come out to monitor the search. She was feeling a little put-upon today."

"I'll probably turn the team loose on it and do some other work. Where do you see this going next?"

"We need to make the rounds of everyone in the county related to the Greaves. He may be holed up with family somewhere."

"That's a definite," she said. "His prints were all over the cartridge."

"That would seem to lead back toward the timber being the motive."

"Maybe," she murmured. "Unless the Greaves knew about the coins."

"Seems unlikely. Nettie hated the guys. But we can ask when we find him."

"Is he related to many down there?'

"Lots, if you count distantly. Close relatives? Half a dozen families."

"And they'd harbor him?"

"Some might, depending on what he gives them as his story."

"And staying clear of the city bitch who shot LJ might convince them?"

I chuckled. "You must know some of Verl's kin."

"It's not just a rural thing," she said. "I know neighborhoods in St. Louis where we'd run into the same thing."

"Yeah," I agreed. "A general high regard for the law."

I shifted to what had been sifting through my brain during my drive around the county and as I'd microwaved a plateful of frozen shrimp for dinner.

"What would you think of a quick trip to Mexico?"

"You mean for you? Me? Or us?"

"I was thinking us."

She was silent for a moment, then said, "To check on the sale of the Indian Princess?"

"Yeah. I did a little more poking around on the web. Five 1861-Ds have been auctioned by this place in Mazatlán, the only five that have been on the market since the 2014 sale I told you about. They were private sales, so I couldn't learn anything about the prices. But they had to have come from Nettie."

"That's a pretty big inference."

I sniffed into the phone. "A damn solid inference. Nettie had no other source of income we can find. She had a supply of the 1861-Ds and was purchasing everything with new hundred dollar bills. And these showed up on the market the year after she retired from the cafeteria."

"Why did she wait 'til then to sell any?"

"She probably didn't need to and may have been a little nervous about taking them public. Not sure who really owned them. That's why she had the library do the search."

"Who do you think does own them? They were stolen from

the Confederacy, then from a Union wagon train."

"I've no idea," I confessed. "The California case suggests she did. But we need to establish that the ones being sold were hers. That's why I think a trip to Mexico is needed."

She was again silent for a moment, then, "Why not take Grace? She speaks fluent Spanish."

"I'd rather go with you. And you're the chief state investigator. Plus, someone needs to be in charge here while I'm gone, and I wouldn't trust things to Frankie or D'Amico."

"I'm not sure we could justify both of us going down there."

"Probably not. But I think it would help if both of us were there. I thought I'd call the seller, tell them I'm an interested bidder but would like to inspect the coin before the sale. If we show as a couple it will be more convincing."

"And leave Officer Torres to do all the grunt work again while you run out of town with me? That will make you popular."

"This murder is our case. And I think I could talk one of the retired police officers in town into stepping back into a deputy role for a few days while I'm gone. That would give Grace some help. He's still around town and was a good lawman."

"And you explain my going by . . .?"

"I don't explain your going. Would the State support you going down?"

"Probably not. Especially if they knew you were making the trip."

Just as I'd figured. But I'd decided to ask anyway. "Could you take a couple of days off and go along? Or you could go as the investigator, and I'd take a couple of vacation days."

I thought for a moment that she'd hung up. "You still there?"

"Yes. I'm thinking about this. It's sounding more like an out-of-country rendezvous than an investigation."

"It's no more than we make it. I think I need to go check this out and believe I'd benefit from having you there with me."

"When are you thinking of going?"

"Flying down Sunday. Back Tuesday. There are direct flights from Dallas. I'll probably leave from Northwest Arkansas. You could come from Springfield."

"You've been thinking this through."

"Yes, I have. I'm planning to go Sunday. I'd like to have you with me."

There was quiet again, but I knew she was still there. "I'll let you know tomorrow," she said finally. "Better go now," and she hung up.

While the team from the state patrol began to work its way through Verl and LJ's hoard, Joseph and I started looking for Verl. His sister lived in Lakeview Estates, a ring of fifteen homes built around an eleven-acre pond out northeast of town. The houses were some of the nicest in the county, built using one of five floorplans offered by Davis-Lauderdale, a developer out of Springfield. When Darleen Greaves had walked out on LJ twenty years ago, she'd taken their only daughter Becky with her. Somehow the girl had survived high school being related to Verl and had gone on to finish the dental hygiene program up at Ozarks Technical College. The day after she graduated, she'd married one of the Lauderdale boys who'd been enrolled in a building trades internship program. He'd talked his father into investing in Lakeview and the couple had made a bundle of money selling lots and building "custom" homes to a commuter set looking for country living. Doug and Becky were good people. I knew they'd chase Verl off with a stick if he showed up at their door. But Becky also would know where else to look, and I'd just as soon start the day with someone friendly.

Grace and Rocky had joined the team from the state at the Greaves warren. They'd be tied up all day. Deputy Ritter had

118

orders to cover everything else unless something major came up. Anything requiring the use of a weapon, he was to call me.

Joseph didn't say a word about Mexico as we drove out to the estate. Becky Lauderdale invited us in like she'd been expecting us and perched us on a cream-colored sofa looking out over the lake at an identical custom-built home that faced us two hundred yards away on the opposite shore. Just what you'd want in secluded country living. I introduced Joseph, and she sat stone silent while I small-talked with Becky about family and life in general before seeing what she could tell me about her brother.

"How's your mother getting on?"

Darleen had been in Chase Backman's care center for over a year, too far down the Alzheimer's road to know who Becky was, and needing more care than her daughter could provide. From what I'd heard, LJ had never been to visit the woman.

"I'm down to working three days a week and spend part of the other four sitting with her. She loves to tell stories to anyone who'll listen. Doesn't know who I am, but I'm a good ear."

"Maybe a good thing, with all the trouble going on. You heard about Verl?"

"Word flies, Tate. You know that."

"You seen him, by chance?"

Becky's smile was sad and cynical at the same time.

"He's as likely to show up at your place as mine," she sniffed. "Verl's mean and hot-tempered. But he's also as smart as an old badger and will have gone to ground just as deep. You won't find him anywhere in the county."

"Not even with your people over along Huckleberry Ridge?" I knew them all. They'd been my neighbors growing up.

"I don't think so, Tate. And he won't have told any of them where he's holed up. He knows you got friends over there, and he's not got many. He wouldn't chance someone ratting him out."

"If he did get in touch with someone, maybe to get some cash or stock up on what he needed to drop out of sight, who would it be?"

"You know them as well as I do, Tate. Charlie. Maybe Packy Durbin. But like I say, he'll know you'll be going right to those people."

"Not Packy," I said. "He's being held over in Tulsa for cutting a guy with a bottle in a bar fight. Been over there most of two weeks."

"See? You know more about what's going on in the family than I do."

"Well, I think I'll run out there and make sure Verl hasn't moved into Packy's place while he's away."

"Be careful, Tate. When you put on that badge, you quit being part of the ridge runners."

"Who are the ridge runners?" Joseph asked as we cut across north of town, past Darnell's studio and my place, and turned down into the southeast corner of the county.

"That's what we used to call ourselves. The kids growing up along Huckleberry Ridge. 'Til I was about twelve, we'd group up after school, grab our 410s or .22s, and go looking to see what we could shoot."

"Like what?"

"Squirrels. Possums. Turkeys. Sometimes a deer."

"Without a license?"

I glanced over to see if she was teasing or if she could really be that naively serious. What I saw was naively sincere. I decided to scrape a little of it off her.

"Out where I grew up, the law was just something people in the city needed to settle their squabbles because they lived too close to each other. I can't think of any law we really took too seriously."

It was her turn to decide if I was being serious. "You're kidding, of course?"

"Nope. Weren't there some laws you all just chose to ignore over there in University City?"

Her brow wrinkled and she stared ahead through the windshield. "I honestly can't think of one, except maybe crossing against the light when no cars were coming."

"Wow. And you're free to tell about it?"

"Don't mock me," she said indignantly. "You come spend some time with me in the city and see if you're right on top of everything."

She was right. I'd spent my share of city time and had made more blunders than I cared to remember. I nodded an apology. "Sorry. That wasn't fair to you. But I only tease people I really like. And I wanted you to be prepared for Huckleberry Ridge. I don't think there's a place out there on a permanent foundation. A few still have outhouses and water from a pump."

"And you grew up out there?"

"Til I went away to college."

"Any family there now?"

"Extended family. My father was killed cutting trees when I was a kid. Mom died while I was in the service. Those that are left aren't close enough that we get together."

"Are you related to the Greaves?"

"Not directly. But connected through an aunt by marriage." It was my turn to stare through the windshield while she watched to see if I was going to say more. When I didn't, she said, "I'll go to Mexico with you."

I looked over to see if that meant more than "I'll go to Mexico with you." I couldn't tell.

"I'm glad. It'll make the trip a lot more enjoyable."

"Separate rooms," she said, clearing up part of my

wondering.

"Of course." I grinned over at her. "Same hotel?"

"I'll be fine with that. But I'm flying down from Springfield. Taking a few vacation days. As far as the state's concerned, you're the official representative on this little outing and going alone."

"I'll make a reservation this afternoon. Let you know what flight I'll be on from Dallas."

"And you can find a hotel," she said. "Let me know what it is and I'll book myself. We don't want it showing up on any receipt."

"I'm glad," I said, and started working out the best way to break the news to the office.

20

There are one hundred and seventy-nine miles of unpaved road in the county. Eleven of them wind through a forest of shortleaf pine, oak, and shag-bark hickory along a crestline that for as long as anyone can remember has been called Huckleberry Ridge. Halfway down the ridge into Durbin Holler, named after my mother's family who settled there a couple of decades before the Civil War, there was once a line of springs that poured out of the hillside just above the bedrock. Most have since dried up, except after a week of downpour when they gush again for a few days as what we call wet-weather springs. Homesteaders built their cabins close to where they could get to one of these sources of good water. As the springs dried up, so did the homesteads. Seven homes still cling to life along the ridge or, I guess I should say, seven semi-inhabited excuses for dwellings. The place I grew up in isn't one of them.

I pulled off the main strip of gravel onto an overgrown lane, stopped short of a gate in a broken fence held closed by a loop of barbed wire hung loosely over a hedgeapple post. Joseph sat in silence taking a measure of the woods beyond the fence while I pushed the gate open.

She gave me an inquisitive side-stare as I climbed back into the car. "Doesn't look like anyone's been down this track in a long time."

I nodded. "Probably not." I eased the cruiser through some blackberry brambles and around a turn in the screen of pines, stopped, but left the car idling. In front of us, what remained of a weather-beaten clapboard shack peeked at us over a thicket of young cedars that now blocked the drive. The oak shake roof had collapsed at one end, leaving broken rafters sticking up out of the room below like a box of gray kindling. Someone had long ago removed the two front windows, salvaging them for some add-on to a hovel farther along the ridge.

"You think Verl might be hiding out in there?" Joseph asked with more than a trace of skepticism.

"No. I just wanted to show you this place. It was home until I left for college."

Joseph gazed at what remained of the decaying shanty, her brow knitting in disbelief. "You said your father died when you were young . . ."

"Ten," I reminded her.

"And you and your mother lived here until you were, what? Seventeen? Eighteen?"

"Just turned eighteen when I left."

"And your mother continued to live here alone?"

"When I left, she moved down the ridge to live with her brother and his family. Packy's dad."

She continued to squint grimly at the skeleton of a house. "I'm sorry," she murmured finally.

I looked sharply over at her. "What for? I didn't stop here for your pity. I actually feel pretty fortunate to have grown up here. I just wanted you to see that I didn't have to come out of Clayton or Ladue to turn out alright."

"I didn't grow up in Clayton or Ladue," she said testily.

"Right. Exaggeration. I meant *next* to Clayton or Ladue."

"Point taken. You turned out alright." She was quiet for long enough I knew she wasn't going to let it end there. "And what do you know about Clayton or Ladue, anyway? You can't have spent much time in St. Louis."

I gazed off through the trees along the ridgeline. "We're going to be meeting my uncle Jack in a few minutes. After my dad died, the one luxury Jack permitted himself and my cousins was two or three road trips to St. Louis to see the

Cardinals play. He usually hauled me along. For Jack, it was something like a sacred pilgrimage to worship at the shrine of Busch Stadium." I grinned back over at her. "And then we'd all go out to Blueberry Hill on the Delmar Loop for a burger. All the way out there we'd listen to Jack sing or tell stories about seeing Chuck Berry there when he was younger. I still remember all the words to *Roll Over Beethoven* and *Johnny B. Goode.*"

"That's still not Clayton or Ladue," she argued.

"Yes. But close enough. We'd cut through there on our way back to the road home so Jack could show us where 'the other half' live."

Joseph sniffed. "You're starting to sound like you *do* want a little pity."

"No. Just wanted you to see that a kid could grow up in a place like this and still do alright."

She glanced back over her shoulder. "That's why we're out here looking for Verl? I'm anxious to see how the rest of the neighborhood fared."

I couldn't suppress a chuckle. "Okay. So maybe there weren't many of us," I conceded and threw the SUV into reverse.

Packy was called Packy because he was the first kid along the ridge to discover that the Sinclair station out on the highway had acquired a used Pac-Man arcade game. Packy had the quick Durbin hands, a knack for seeing the whole screen, and an eye that could drop a squirrel with a .22 at fifty yards. By the time the rest of us figured out where he was running off to by himself after school, he'd become so good at the game the rest of us never could beat the kid. His place was the next stop along the ridge.

"Aside from having windows and a roof that isn't caved in, this place looks pretty much the same," Joseph muttered under her breath, but loud enough she knew I would hear.

"May be the same windows," I agreed. "He moved out of his parents' place about the time Mom left ours."

"Does anyone ever bother to paint?"

I shrugged. "You'll see that Uncle Jack's place is painted. But Packy? He'd never paint. Too expensive and a waste of time."

"From what you told Becky, it sounds like he has a pretty busy schedule," Joseph said cynically.

I couldn't let that pass. "Now, there's a big city comment. A waste of time doesn't mean he's got a lot of other pressing things to do. Just that he'd rather do something else—or nothing—more than he wants to paint."

Joseph sniffed. "You sound like you sympathize with that kind of thinking."

"I not only sympathize, I sometimes practice it," I called back to her, swinging out of the car and heading toward the door.

No one had been at Packy's. The door was unlocked. The window in the front living space was pulled up about four inches and a light dusting covered the plank floor. No footprints.

I took a quick look inside from the doorsill, walked to the back and did the same at the kitchen door, then joined Joseph who was peering through the single side window into the bedroom.

"There's practically no furniture in there." She said it as if this was going to be some great revelation.

"No more than a single guy needs."

"And there's a wash basin on a side table."

"No running water in the house."

"Where does he get it?"

"There's still live water here, about thirty yards down the hill."

"Live water?"

126

"Yeah. I mean a spring that still flows."

"And the bathroom. . . ?"

"About twenty feet in the other direction. You want to keep the john away from the spring."

"That must be cold as hell in the winter."

I grinned over at her. "Here, you don't go out there to read."

Jack Tate heard the grate of tires on gravel and met us on the front porch, a Cardinals cap pulled down loosely over his shock of gray hair. He gave Joseph a long, appraising look, then turned his attention to his only nephew.

"Looks like an official visit, Colby, with the trooper lady."

"Afraid so, Jack. This is Officer Mara Joseph." They exchanged nods. "We're checking to see if Verl's come out here to hide out with some of his kin."

Jack scowled, his eyes hardening. "We heard he might have taken a shot at your lady friend. But why you stopping here, Colby? You know Verl's not welcome out here. He, or that excuse for a father of his."

I nodded and tried to look like I knew that all along. "That's what I told Officer Joseph. But I also told her you'd know if he was hanging around here anywhere."

Jack looked critically again at my partner, as if trying to decide how much family talk she should be privy to.

"He hasn't been nowhere out here in months," he said finally. "Charlie and me was over at Lloyd's place just this mornin', helpin' him pull a calf that needed to be turned. Lloyd hadn't seen him since the start of the summer and was damn certain he'd know he better not show his face along the ridge."

"I figured as much. But had to check. How's Shirley? And how's Charlie getting on?" Charlie had come back from his stint in the Marines with a heavy dose of PTSD, brought on by being the only one in his gun truck to survive an IED blast. He'd been virtually untouched, and it was eating away at him.

Some days he was his old self. A devil-may-care screw-off who figured the world didn't owe him a thing, and he didn't owe it anything in return. Other days, he was so tortured I thought he'd have been better off to be taken with the rest of his squad.

"He has his days," Jack said grimly. "He's still over with Lloyd. He'd get some help from seein' more of you."

Jack was right and I knew it. When Charlie was in bad shape, I was about the only old friend left around who had any idea what he'd been through. But I didn't like to relive it either and too often left Charlie to face his demons on his own.

"I'll do better," I promised Jack and believed I would. "Well, we'll be getting on. Hug Shirley for me and tell Charlie I'll be calling him about fishing. Call me if you hear anything about Verl."

Jack nodded in such a way that I could tell he wasn't sure I'd be calling Charlie. We walked back to the patrol car.

"You believe him?" Joseph asked.

"Completely. He wouldn't lie to me."

"Things seemed a little strained."

"If you hadn't been along and I was here just as family, it would have been completely different."

"Tough being sheriff when you know everybody."

"And are related to half of everybody. But the good thing about it is, as long as you do the job right, they tell you things just the way they are."

We turned the Explorer in the drive and headed back up toward the road.

"So, what's this pulling a calf?" Joseph wanted to know.

"It was coming breach. They had to reach in and turn it."

Joseph cringed. "Is this something you could do?"

"I've helped with it. Jack's the pro. He's as good with cattle as any of the vets around."

"And Charlie? What's up with Charlie?"

I told her about the IED blast.

"Damn," she murmured. "I can only imagine . . ."

"No," I assured her. "You really can't."

21

We stopped at LeeAnn's on the way back to the office to get a quick lunch: a Reuben for me and a club for Joseph. It gave her a chance to see small-town law enforcement up close and personal. Our table was midway down the wall between the door and the register. Coming or going, everyone in the café passed us. Most stopped.

"How's it going, Tate?" was the standard greeting, with a hand extended toward me and a sidelong glance and nod at a patrol officer who didn't look like any they'd seen before. "Getting any breaks on Nettie's case?"

"Making progress," I'd say, and they'd say, "Terrible thing" or "I hope you get the sonofabitch."

Joseph leaned over between supporters and whispered, "It must be nice. Knowing everyone and having them rooting for you."

"Most of the time," I agreed. "But everybody in here already knows you were shot at, that we have people going through the Greaves place this morning, and that you and I have been visiting the folks out on Huckleberry Ridge. Sometimes a little more secrecy would be nice."

"How do they find out so quickly?"

I grinned across at her. "Information's the coin of the realm in a town like this. Jerry rules supreme because he knows almost everything. Knowing something before someone else does and letting them know it—that makes for a satisfying day. Someone headed into town along the ridge road saw us parked at Uncle Jack's, knew I was with the state patrol woman, and stopped at the market or by the bank. Think of it as hitting

"Post" on your Facebook page."

A wiry kid who smelled of ground oats and molasses stopped and looked Joseph over more directly than the older set had been willing to do. "How's it going, Tate? Did you turn up anything out at Verl's place?"

"Just on our way to the office to find out," I said. "We don't have any reason right now to think the Greaves were involved."

"Except them cuttin' Nettie's timber," the kid said. "Well anyway, I hope you catch the sonofabitch done this to her."

Joseph arched her brows and leaned forward, following him with her eyes as he left the café. "Interesting smell," she whispered. "I couldn't place it."

"Randy works the dock at the feed store," I explained. "Loads bags of stock feed all day."

"Hmm," she murmured. "I kind of like it."

Grace and two state officers had a folding table set up against one wall of the office, covered by an arsenal more impressive than we had in our munitions cabinet. Three semi-automatic rifles, five shotguns of various gauges, an assortment of handguns, and hundreds of rounds of ammunition. No Marlin. But as we entered, Grace held up a lever-action rifle with a gloved hand.

"You got here just in time. We found a Winchester model 94. I was about to go fire a test round and send the cartridge back with the state people to check against the one you found."

"Let them take the rifle," I suggested. "I'd just as soon they have custody during the test-firing, and they can do the printing at the same time. But I doubt that's the weapon."

She nodded. "Yup. No scope. And that was a pretty good shot from the road. I'm guessing Verl used his Marlin. He reclaimed it on the way out." She waved an arm over the table. "But they had quite a collection in there without it."

I walked to the table to look over the weapons. "I'm surprised you could find anything in there. Were there other boobytraps?"

A state policeman whose nametag said Corporal Doniphan was pulling copies off the printer and handed me the top sheet. "Here's a preliminary report. There was one guarding the back entrance as well. Rigged just like the front. They had a simple hook that could be attached across the passageways they'd created. We believe they unfastened them when in the house. They probably hooked them both up when they went out to meet you two coming down the hill. And the weapons? The only organized place in the whole building was a six-foot gun cabinet in the back part of the building. There were a couple of beds back there with junk piled right up against them on two sides. This cabinet was right beside the back door where they could get to it in a hurry."

Joseph glanced over the sheet, turning it over to find the back blank. "You don't say much about what was in all those piles. You couldn't have had time this morning to sort through all that junk."

Doniphan straightened and shifted his gun belt, looking to Grace and his partner for support. "We were tasked with checking the place out for boobytraps. We brought the weapons in because we identified the place as a crime scene and because of the shot from the ridge. I don't think there was any expectation that we'd go through all that junk. Just from a pretty thorough walk-through, it looked to us like those guys collected anything and everything someone else had thrown away. There were TV sets, old vacuums, plastic yard ornaments, bicycle parts. You name it. What was it you were wanting us to look for?"

"He's right," Grace cut in, taking a step toward the patrolman as if he might need to fend off a charge. "The place was full of crap. It smelled like dead mice and sweaty sheets and, without some specific reason, there wasn't anything to be gained by hauling all that stuff outside. There wasn't room in there to just shift it around."

Joseph looked at the chief deputy thoughtfully for a moment, then nodded. "I guess you're right. If the place is secured, we can always go back." The two women stood and looked at each other without expression for long enough that I figured I'd better intervene.

"What did you learn about the bruises on the kids and from Maria Hernandez?"

Grace kept her eyes on Joseph for another few seconds, then turned and walked to her desk. "As usual, Maria withdrew her complaint when I showed up. I told her again that we could help her find a shelter if she ever needed a safe place to stay. She didn't look convinced. I checked the kids over and thought the school was right to be concerned. We brought social services in and took them by the clinic to be checked. The case worker stayed with them and is going to follow up."

I saw my opening. "Good work. And while I'm thinking of it, you're going to need to take care of things here for a few days. I'm taking a quick trip down to Mexico on Sunday to see if I can trace some of that evidence I talked to you about." Grace immediately shot a glance back at Joseph. I pulled the reservation copy from my jacket pocket and handed it to Marti. "Can you run a reimbursement request through for me? I've booked a flight to Mazatlán from Northwest Arkansas and will be back Tuesday afternoon."

Grace shifted her gaze back to me, then down at the notes she'd taken about the bruised children. "Yeah, I can take care of things here. Will I be escorting the state investigator around while you're away?"

Joseph answered for me. "I have plenty to keep me busy until the sheriff gets back. The place is all yours."

22

Joseph asked if I'd ever been to Mexico. We were sitting at Gate B 21 at Dallas/Fort Worth waiting for an 11:47 a.m. departure to Mazatlán. I had been to Mexico but had to think for a minute before deciding what to tell her. Every Marine I knew at the Corp's San Diego Recruit Depot had been to Mexico. Or at least they had been as far as Zona Norte in Tijuana where the women lined up against the faded plaster walls and corrugated roll-down doors of seedy clubs like so many faded Barbies in a secondhand store window. I'd gone with my buddies a few times. Had never sampled the Barbies. I was still under the saving influence of my mother's strict Southern Baptist upbringing and scared to death of coming home with one of the many crotch-ravaging conditions that seemed endemic in the barracks. But I did take in a few shows that would have curdled our preacher's urine and wasn't sure how much Joseph needed to know.

"Yes," I finally conceded. "But only down into the border towns when I was in the service."

"Marines? That would be Tijuana," she guessed. "I was thinking more of *real* Mexico."

"I guess not, then. And what would *real* Mexico include?"

"Some place where regular Mexicans live."

"I think I was seeing real Mexicans."

"Yeah. Like Mustang Ranch is real America."

"And like you've been to Mustang Ranch?"

She shot me a "You're tap dancing around my question" look and said, "So, I take it the answer is no."

"Have *you* been to real Mexico, then?"

She nodded in such a way that I knew the whole thing had been leading up to my asking that question. "My family used to spend part of the summer each year in San Miguel de Allende. Frankly, that's one of the reasons I decided to take you up on this invitation."

I gave her a disappointed frown. "And I was thinking it was my irresistible charm."

"That was one of the other reasons," she grinned back at me.

"And this San Miguel de Allende. That's real Mexico, I gather?"

"There are tons of expats there from all over, but it's a beautiful old colonial city. And yes, I'd say it's real Mexico."

"Do you speak Spanish?"

"Well enough to get around."

"Great. Then you're in charge, once we get to Mazatlán. Unless we run into a delegation from one of the Arabian states. Then I'll take over."

"I think Mazatlán will be different. It's on the Pacific coast. San Miguel is inland. About the middle of the country."

"Close enough," I said with a slight shrug. "They'll still speak Spanish, won't they? So you're in charge."

She rolled her eyes and started to make some smart retort, but stopped to hear the gate announcement. "That's us," she said. "You want window or aisle?"

I grabbed the backpack that held my 'if my bags don't make it' change of socks and underwear. "Back in steerage, tall men always want the aisle," I told her.

Mazatlán *was* different. The airport is twenty minutes south of the city, and the mountain side of the drive into town was nothing but parched fields of thorny, head-high brush. On the ocean side, shells of what looked like resorts-gone-bankrupt lined the highway like so many Mayan ruins, suggesting the city had seen better days. The blazing sun reminded me of

Dubai, and beyond a long strip of coastal buildings, the ocean gleamed silver-gray.

I had arranged for a car and driver through a company called King David. The driver was a fiftyish man with a dark suit stretched over an ample paunch and official-looking chauffeur's cap. Joseph's running conversation with the man showed more than a passing facility with Spanish. I quickly learned how my Marine buddies felt when I was jabbering away in Pashto and they had no idea what I was talking about. I recognized "Don Pelayo Pacific Beach," the place I'd arranged for us to stay, but the rest was—well, like Spanish to me.

"Wanna share?" I knew I sounded as irritated as I felt.

"I'm asking about good places to eat and what he recommends."

"So, what's for dinner?"

"There's a place near the hotel called Chili's Pepper. Right on the beach. He says it has some of the best *molcajete* in the city."

"Okay. What's *molcajete*?"

"You ever seen those three-legged Mexican lava bowls? That's what a *molcajete* is. Chili's cooks up a stew in them Gabriel says shouldn't be missed."

"So, you've got dinner plans for us?"

"You said I was in charge. What were you thinking? A Big Mac or a visit to the Colonel? They'll have both here somewhere."

She was right. As we entered the city proper, I began to wonder if the failed resorts had just been ill-conceived efforts to build too far out. Brand name big-box retailers lined divided avenues that streamed with late-model cars. Every tenth face was an expat: pale, pudgy men in knee-length shorts, gaudy tropical shirts, and spanking new Panama hats shuffled along the walks with their dutiful wives three paces behind. And sure enough. There were the golden arches and KFC.

The Don Pelayo was a towering white beachfront palace that looked more Mediterranean than Mayan. My room was creamy pink, the marble-topped desk and wall table molded out of the same concrete that formed the floor and walls. No one was going to walk away with the Don Pelayo's furniture. A pink veranda overlooked a turquoise pool with a waterslide twisting down through a very natural-looking pile of rock. I'd stayed in places this fancy in Dubai and felt like a toad in an aquarium full of angel fish. But this one had a more natural feel to it, maybe because the couch and desk were poured concrete and I could hear a pretty good Mariachi band playing down by the pool. The seductive tang of refried beans and salsa wafted up from somewhere below. I hadn't eaten anything but a bag of pretzels since leaving home.

Joseph stepped onto the balcony next to mine, dressed in shorts that matched the blue of the pool below and a soft, white silk shirt. She smiled over at me, and I had to gulp a breath to keep my heart in check. I'd seen her wet in the creek and tightly packed into her state patrol uniform, but never with full makeup looking quite this womanly. Damn near beautiful when she wanted to be.

"You feeling like dinner?" she asked, her face coloring at the flush she could see on mine.

"I just need a minute to change." I'd thrown a couple of pairs of shorts in my bag. But mine were more L.L. Bean with a dozen pockets. I wasn't sure they'd even been pressed. The extra shirts both had logos over the pocket. Shelter Cove Resort. Indian Springs B&G. Better suited to a safari than a night out with the sexiest woman I'd been with since coming back to the Ozarks. I at least had a pair of loafers I could wear without socks, giving me some semblance of resort cool.

During the quarter-mile stroll to the restaurant we passed more tourists than natives, and I had to wonder again if this was real Mexico. Most were dressed with much less concern about public appearance than I had, and Joseph didn't seem uncomfortable walking beside me. I knew we looked like a couple, a pretty nice-looking couple, and I liked that.

Chili's Pepper was at the end of a corridor cut through a collection of T-shirt and souvenir shops, folk art galleries, and places renting boogie boards and beach umbrellas. The restaurant was open on three sides and overlooked a wide stretch of white sand and evening-gray ocean. A couple of rocky islands blocked the sun as it dove toward the western horizon, leaving our table against the railing in the cool, half-light of a salmon Mexican sunset. Families and gaggles of young singles partied beneath striped umbrellas along the beach. Grandparents lounged in plastic deck chairs and children chased after black-capped gulls that launched raids in twos and threes against the remains of picnics.

Joseph stretched lazily. "Gabriel was right," she murmured. "This is a beautiful, romantic place to spend an evening."

"You asked him about romantic places?"

She smiled mischievously. "He volunteered. Thought we were a couple."

I gave her a little head nod, not wanting to ruin the fantasy with some lame comment. She ordered a Margarita and I a local Pacifico. It came with a saucer of salt and slices of fresh lime. We both ordered the *molcajete* and Joseph added something that sounded from my vague memory of high school Spanish like it was called "three milks."

"It's a surprise," she assured me. "And you'll love it."

The *molcajete* lived up to its billing. The black lava bowl sizzled with a soup of sliced beef, thick-cut bacon, onions, peppers, mushrooms, tomato sauce, greens, avocado, and a coating of tangy white cheese. A savory vapor of cocoa, cumin, and chili hung over the bowl and my saliva glands opened to the point I had to wipe at my mouth to keep from drooling. We had asked for "medium" on the chili scale and Joseph sipped at the broth without a blink. The first spoonful slipped easily down my throat, then began to smolder its way back up to the tip of my tongue. I doused the flame with the Pacifico, gave my system a chance to turn on the fire suppressors, and dove back in. I hadn't enjoyed a dish this much since leaving the Middle East. Or maybe it was the company.

The "three milks" turned out to be a multi-layered, cream-filled cake with which some master baker had managed to find that perfect point between moist and soggy. Ambrosia to the taste buds!

"Incredible," I managed to mumble through a mouthful. Joseph's laugh showed flirty delight. Candles now glowed in the center of the tables and the flame kindled gold embers in her dark eyes.

During the walk back to Don Pelayo, a magnetic pull wanted to draw our hands together, but neither of us was willing to allow the first touch. At her door I said, "This has been a perfect evening. Best I've had in many years."

"It has," she agreed and waited, looking up at me just long enough to give me hope, then dropped her eyes in what I read to be resignation, squeezed my hand to say "Nice thought, but better not," and slipped alone into her room.

23

Mazatlán Numismatics was in the old part of town, what definitely would have qualified as "Real Mexico." We rode into the city along a mile-long curve of white sand in what the locals called a *pulmonia*, a souped-up golf cart-looking jitney with an open canopy roof and a sound system that could churn butter.

"From what the driver tells me, these are unique to Mazatlán," Joseph yelled over a hundred decibel rendition of some Latin chart topper. "They're built on old VW bug frames. The name literally means 'pneumonia,' I guess because of all the fumes we're sucking in. They're cheaper than a taxi, and faster than the bus."

"I'll spring for a taxi on the way back," I shouted, but she was watching fishing boats unload their morning catch along a makeshift pier. My offer disappeared into a throbbing bass from woofers the size of microwaves that hung just behind our heads. She had dressed again in shorts, her morning choice a loose khaki with a brightly flowered blouse. There was enough room on the vinyl seat for three to pack in tightly or two to sit without touching. She chose to slide close enough that our arms brushed. We both pretended not to notice.

Angel Flores Street climbed away from the bay into the old city over a gradual hill, lined shoulder-to-shoulder on both sides by arched, Spanish-style homes in pinks, pastel blues, ochre, and Indian red. A walk fronted the houses, raised above the sunken street to chest-height and separated from traffic by heavy concrete balusters. As the street descended into the heart of Old Mazatlán, some of the homes yielded space to narrow-fronted specialty shops with small living quarters above.

The single window in the shop selling rare coins offered an array of Central and South American specimens perched on plexiglass racks. Decorative cast iron grating covered the full pane of window glass, far enough from the treasures that an arm reaching through a broken pane couldn't reach the display. I scanned the coins for US currency, finding only a row of buffalo-head nickels.

Inside the shop, a long glass-topped counter stretched from the right of the door to an exit in the rear wall, cutting the room in half. When we entered, a chime jingled overhead and a hunched little man with a gray fringe surrounding a bald, chocolate-colored dome hurried through the back curtain. He was perfect for the part, with eyes magnified to twice normal size by thick, wire-rimmed glasses.

"*Hablas Ingles?*" I asked before Joseph could launch into a conversation in Spanish. I wanted to hear all of this one firsthand.

The man strained unsuccessfully to force the curve from his back, peering up at me with an amused grin. "I speak English very well, though with a bit of an Arkansas accent."

"We should understand each other well, then," I said. "I hail from just north of the border."

He allowed his head to relax forward. "Mexican border or Arkansas border?"

"Arkansas border. About thirty miles into Missouri."

His bent head wagged more side-to-side than up-and-down. "Very good. My name's Pogue. Rufus Pogue. Can I interest you in some out-of-circulation currency? I have everything from souvenir coins and bills to investment grade gold and silver."

"I contacted you by email about the Confederate gold dollar you advertised. The1861-D. I asked if I could come have a look at it."

"Ah, yes. Mr. Tate."

"The same. And this is my friend Mara. There are a lot of Pogues up our way. Do you have kin in Missouri?" I realized as I said it that all the Pogues I knew were white, but it was too late to turn back, and they might be related anyway.

He knew more about the Pogues than I did. "Yes. We're related. But not closely. I wouldn't know any of them." He wasn't any more interested in tracing the genealogy than I was. "What questions about the dollar can I answer for you?"

"Would it be possible for us to examine the coin?"

"Of course. Let me lock the shop while we look at it. I would prefer we go into the back and don't wish to leave the front unattended."

"Not a problem," I agreed. The little man lifted a section of counter and shuffled through to twist a deadbolt into place on the metal door.

"Now, if you will follow me into the back." He held up the counter flap while I ushered Joseph through, then scurried ahead to hold back the curtain. I wondered that he would trust us alone in a locked shop with such a valuable treasure until we stepped through the narrow doorway. A much younger man, easily my size but with twenty pounds of extra bulk, all solid, sat in a formed plastic chair beside a desk. He gazed without looking away at a muted Mexican version of *Dancing with the Stars* on a flat screen mounted on the opposite wall. He was a good looking guy, probably early twenties, and easily could have passed for any of the two hundred young immigrant men who were the lifeblood of the poultry farms and chicken processing plants that lined the state line south of Crayton. Except for the eyes. Cold and remote as black Mexican onyx.

"My security man, Miguel," the Arkansan said, twisting to try unsuccessfully to grin back over his shoulder. "When we first set up shop here about ten years ago, we had an attempt a week to free us of some of our more desirable merchandise. As you probably know, we are in Sinaloa State here, home to one of the more notorious cartels in the country. For a monthly fee, they now provide us with security. We had an attempted theft about three months ago, our first in several years. Miguel didn't even have to manhandle the stupid kids. He just said a few words and they ran like a couple of scared rabbits."

Had we had dishonorable intentions, the explanation would have been enough to keep us from trying anything foolish. Miguel continued to stare at the muted screen, letting us know by his disinterest that he wasn't someone to trifle with. I suspected he only left the chair if he heard trouble.

Other than the desk beside the guard, the back room had a wall safe the size of a double refrigerator, a small table with two chairs on one side and one on the other, and Miguel. Mr. Pogue indicated the two chairs, waited until we were seated, then blocked the dial with his bent body while he spun in the combination. From an upper shelf, he retrieved a square plastic case that he brought back to the table and placed in its center.

Had Joseph and I not recently run our hands through a small pile of the cold coins, just the appearance of the dollar would have shrieked *priceless*. The metal's sheen was as bright as the day it was minted and seemed to catch every beam that emanated from the three-bulb fixture that hung over the table. I bent low to look at the Princess side, confirming that the U in United States hadn't minted cleanly, what I had read to be one of the signature indicators of a genuine 1861-D. Of the estimated 1250 that were minted, fewer than fifty recovered coins had been certified as genuine. There was good reason to be skeptical. I spoke while still staring down at the gold face of the Indian woman.

"I noticed in your catalog that you've had one of these available for auction about every year for the past four or five years. How do you verify that they're not fakes? For the prices these bring, someone could forge one out of pure gold and still make one hell of a profit."

The old man chuckled. "How much do you really want to

know? I can give you the long answer or the short answer."

"How about the medium answer?"

"Okay. Short answer with a little more explanation. We can quickly assay the gold to determine karat. That would eliminate some fakes quickly since we know the karat of authentic 1861-D gold coins. A very skilled forger could duplicate the gold content, but these coins were minted using an old obverse die of the 1860-D gold dollar. I see from your examination that you know there were flaws in that die. It is very difficult for even a master forger to exactly duplicate those flaws. Am I being brief enough?"

"You say 'very difficult.' But not impossible?"

"Not impossible. But the third test moves us into that territory." He craned his neck upward to peer at Joseph, thinking she might need more explanation than I did. "The D on an 1861-D is for a branch mint established in Dahlonega, Georgia. In the 1860s, there was gold being mined in the south, mainly in Georgia, Virginia, and the Carolinas. It was too risky to move that gold to Philadelphia where the main mint was, so the government set up branch mints, this one in Georgia." With Joseph appropriately schooled, Pogue shifted his attention back to the coin. "Gold mined in different locations has different trace elements present in the samples, even when highly refined. We know from spectroscopic analysis done on several coins we are certain were from the 1861 Dahlonega minting that the gold came from mines in Georgia and South Carolina. There hasn't been mining in those states since World War II. So it would be virtually impossible for a forger to get gold with the right trace elements. Our coins have tested perfectly."

"That testing doesn't damage the coins?" Joseph asked, picking up the case and turning it carefully against the overhead light.

"It's a laser test that's microscopic to the point any change in weight wouldn't be measurable with our most sophisticated instruments. I can assure you, this is a genuine '61-D."

His explanation was just the opening I needed for the question we had come to ask. "Can you tell me how you managed to get ahold of these coins? Five authentic dollars in as many years?"

Mr. Pogue turned his head sideways to keep from having to try to straighten. He winked at me slyly. "My son has a source through our shop in the US that I'm not at liberty to divulge."

"Shop in the US?"

"Yes. Not too far from you. Springdale, Arkansas."

Mention of Springdale hit me in the solar plexus like a sucker punch, something I should have seen coming, but was too caught up in the touristy ambiance of Old Town Mazatlán to anticipate.

"Springdale as in Northwest Arkansas?"

"Yes. That's where our home store is."

A glance at Joseph showed that she was right with me and just as embarrassed at having missed the connection.

"So, these have come from your home store in Springdale. Why not market them there?"

Another wink through a thick lens. "Let me just say that there are some significant advantages to doing some of our business out-of-country. And in my declining years, I find the climate here much kinder to my allergies and rheumatism. You couldn't drag me back up there with a team of horses." He lifted the plastic case from the table. "Have you seen what you need to see? Our auction will be live on November 30. I certainly hope you will decide to join us."

I nodded and pushed back from the table. Miguel glanced over just long enough to be certain I wasn't reaching for a piece. Joseph stood with me and extended a hand to the jeweler.

"I'm certainly satisfied," she said. "Colby? Have you been able to ask what you wanted?" There was an intimacy in the way she said "Colby" that I heard as more than just show.

"I'm good, Mara," I said, hoping she heard the same. "And we definitely plan to be part of the auction. You have my email information. Do you happen to have a card for your Springdale shop? It's close enough that we might want to stop in and see what you have there."

The old man's grin broadened. "Our source is very tightly guarded. But you are certainly welcome to go by." He spoke in Spanish to Miguel who pulled open a desk drawer, pulled out a card, and leaned far enough in my direction to hand it to me. I nodded without a *gracias* and slipped it into my shirt pocket. I shook Pogue's hand and we left him to place his treasure back in the safe, under the less-than-watchful eye of his cartel security man.

We walked to the main plaza and detoured through the Cathedral of the Immaculate Conception. Its twin spires and the triple lancet arches of its pale mustard façade struck me as doing exactly what its architect had intended: drew every eye heavenward. They pointed into a sky that on this particular morning was whisked by horsetail clouds into a gauzy azure.

Joseph remained thoughtfully silent until we exited the church. When she finally spoke, it was about food. "There's a lunch spot across the street that's supposed to be fun. Let's find a quiet table."

"How do you know all this? You hardly said anything to the pneumonia driver."

She held up her phone. "Found it this morning before we left the hotel." She led through one of the plaza gates and dodged cars and an unyielding bus across a crowded street that separated the shop from the cathedral. "Their webpage says they have great *tres leche* cake. I thought you'd approve."

The eatery filled a quarter of the next block but screamed calories. Through a wall-sized window, racks of cakes, cookies, and cream-plumped eclairs beckoned to passers-by with seductive success. What looked like a caricature of a surfer with a huge red-lipped smile, cake hat, and plate of cupcakes in one hand rode the waves beside a sign over the entrance that read "Panama Restaurant y Pasteleria."

"I like it already," I yelled, vaulting out of the way of a battered,

Toyota pickup and onto the sidewalk. "Do they serve anything healthy?"

"It's a regular restaurant," she called back, pushing through the glass doors.

Finding a quiet table was not in the cards. Our best chance at privacy came from the general din of the place: animated chatter all around with no one paying any attention to conversation at other tables. A plump hostess in a tight black pantsuit seated us, replaced immediately by a young woman dressed like a waitress from a 1950's diner: short black dress and white apron.

"If you're looking for something healthy," Joseph said, studying the menu, "they have some great fish dishes. And as you saw coming in this morning, this is a fishing port."

I waved at the menu. "You choose for both of us." She ordered two Pacificos and something called *Filete de Pescado San Miguel*. I chuckled. "Is this to honor some saint or our friendly cartel guard this morning?"

She gave me a noncommittal shrug. "We'll see how it tastes."

As the waitress moved on to the next table for an order, Joseph leaned back against the dun padding of the booth seat. "An 1820 *escudo* for your thoughts," she said with a thin smile.

"From what I remember from the shop window, that's pretty pricey thinking."

She cocked her head to one side and waited.

"Well," I offered, "I'd say we just picked up at least two more suspects. Springdale is about an hour's drive from Nettie's place. No farther than Springfield. I have to confess that I was letting the state line limit my thinking about where she might go to sell her coins. But I'll bet you ten 1820 *escudos* that the 1861s sold down here came from her stash."

"I'd say at least *three* new suspects," Joseph suggested. "Maybe all complicit."

"You're including our man Miguel?"

She nodded. "Let's suppose the Pogues learned that Nettie was losing her place through eminent domain and would be moving. They wouldn't know where, and couldn't be sure she would continue doing business with them. They might have decided to try to find her supply before she could take it somewhere else."

"I'd had the same thought."

"And our coin merchant here obviously has some connection, however slight it might be, with the Mexican mob. And employs one of their strongmen."

I nodded. "But I doubt old Rufus Pogue did the job. Could Miguel have made it into the state without being stopped by ICE?"

"We know hundreds are crossing undetected. It's the ones who really want to make an appeal for legal asylum who make sure they get caught. I don't think Miguel would have any trouble getting across and up into the state."

The waitress brought our beers. "We need to see if we can have our unidentified prints from the trailer run through Mexican police files then. See if we get a match on our man Miguel."

"I'll call as soon as we get back to the hotel," Joseph agreed.

I gave her an amused smile. "I think I'd better call. You're just taking a few days off, remember? We don't want the Patrol calling a report from Officer Joseph about Mexican prints back to Crayton."

"I can see why people have trouble getting away with affairs," she said, her own smile tight-jawed. "Okay. You call in the request. What do you want to do about Springdale?"

"I'm flying into Northwest Arkansas from Dallas. I'll just be a couple of miles from Springdale."

Joseph shook her head slowly. "Not without me," she muttered. "I'll get back to Springfield about 2:00 in the afternoon tomorrow. Give me time to get some clean clothes. I'll be down by dinnertime. Are you open to another overnight guest?"

The girl arrived with steaming plates of a white fish with avocado dressing, beans, brown rice, and a small mixed salad. I tried not to sound eager. "Sure. I'd love the company." I took a bite of the fish and avocado. This dish was definitely named after Saint Miguel.

24

Joseph reached the house as I was grilling a side of salmon on a cedar plank, gave three sharp knocks, and again walked in without waiting for an answer. The lemon spices drew her immediately out onto the deck.

"What if you'd found me in a state of undress?" I asked, keeping my back to her as she stepped through the French doors.

"That would be a sight worth the drive," she said lightly. "Anyway, I could smell the salmon when I got out of the car and assumed you might not want to leave it. And I guessed, perhaps a bit rashly, that it was unlikely you barbequed in the nude."

I slid a spatula under the plank and moved it to the side of the grill. "Not a safe assumption out here in the woods. But I was expecting company."

She hesitated, glancing back into the house. "I'm not going to be getting in the way of anything . . .?"

"Not unless you keep me from getting plates on the table. And there should still be some of that Pinot in the fridge. You can grab me a Bud Light."

She was in jeans and a St. Louis Blues T-shirt and looked every bit as good as she had in the shorts. She tossed a small duffle onto my leather recliner and set about readying the table, hunting for what she needed without asking. In the mystery drawer beneath the stove, she found a sauté pan and quickly discovered the olive oil in the lazy Susan in the corner cupboard. She was cutting vegetables into the oil when I carried the salmon to the table. I looked admiringly into the sizzling mix.

"I didn't think I had any peppers and broccoli."

"You didn't. I brought them."

"Very thoughtful."

"I saw the salmon when I was here before and guessed you might have it tonight."

"The skills of a consummate investigator."

"And a woman who knows you don't want to let fish thaw in the fridge for too long."

"Good culinary practice has never been a deterrent. It could have been there for another week if I hadn't had company."

"Not if you opened the fridge very often."

She had been thinking about Mazatlán and wanted to talk as we ate.

"That was a nice little trip. The closest thing to a vacation I've had in five or six years."

Nice is one of those words that can mean a lot of things.

"We should have spent more time," I agreed. "I read about some quaint little Mexican villages that aren't far from there. And there's a famous old theater near the cathedral that would have made a nice evening out. I could have spent another day just walking around the Old Town." In my case, I meant *nice* to mean "a very romantic and intimate time together."

"Hmm," she murmured. "Maybe the case will take us back down there before it's over, and we won't feel like we need to get back so quickly."

I'd been couth enough to pour my Bud into a glass and was mid-sip, almost choking on the swallow. She laughed as I lowered the glass to the table and pulled a napkin up to stifle the cough.

"I take it you weren't expecting that."

"Hoping for, but not expecting."

She reached over and placed a hand on the one that held the glass, giving it a light squeeze. "I've been as interested as you appear to be, Tate. But I had a smart, handsome partner before and let it get personal. It turned out to be a real mess and I swore I'd never let it happen again. I'm trying to be careful."

"You know about Adeena. That was no mess, but I didn't think I'd ever get over the loss. And I'll admit, Mexico was the first time I wished I'd had more time to spend with a woman." I released the glass and turned my hand to squeeze hers. "But my guess is that within minutes of the time we left that shop, a call came up here to Springdale. I don't think Pogue was suspicious of us, but if they were involved in any way in Nettie's death, the old man would want the home office to know someone had been asking questions about where the coins came from, especially two people from Missouri. I felt like we needed to get home."

"Especially since you were supposed to be down there alone," Joseph grinned, giving me another light squeeze and withdrawing her hand. "It wouldn't have been good if old Mr. Pogue had googled Colby Tate, learned that you are a sheriff, then called your office before we got back, asking about the couple who'd visited his shop in Mazatlán." After a moment during which both of us were trying to think of somewhere else to take the conversation, she said, "So, why would Nettie go to Springdale?"

I shrugged. "You're from St. Louis. The cities in Illinois are just as close or closer than many in Missouri, but people just think 'in-state.' It's like you're crossing some magic boundary there when you cross the river to Alton or whatever else is over on the Illinois side. My guess is that Nettie wanted that boundary between her life in the holler and her sales transactions. Keep them in a different world."

"It seems to have worked. We didn't even think of Arkansas."

"Shame on us," I agreed.

The Cardinals were playing the Cubs in Chicago which gave

us a good reason to sit up late, close enough on the sofa to share a bag of microwave popcorn and keep our thoughts on other things. It worked as long as the game was on, but not after we turned in. I tried the tricks that usually lull me off to sleep: creating another imaginary day in Mazatlán, extending it into a shared night at the Don Pelavo, imagining how she would feel if pressed in beside me. It didn't work. She was too close.

As I was lifting my head to peer over the pillow to see how many minutes it had been since it last read 12:43, I heard the soft scrape of the door. She slipped beneath the covers and pulled tightly against my back, her breasts warm and firm against a back that must have felt like a kettle drum in full percussion.

"We'll probably regret this tomorrow," she whispered.

I rolled into her, pulling her hips tightly against mine. "Let's deal with it then," I murmured softly into her hair, her lips nibbling at my neck.

Her laugh was playful. "I see that you've been expecting me."

"Not expecting. Just hoping," I rolled a body onto mine that was as firm and supple as I had fantasized. I eased her back across my hips and stopped imagining.

Springdale, Arkansas stretches along both sides of that piece of I-49 that separates the retirement haven of Bella Vista from the Razorback-crazy university town of Fayetteville. On the north, it bumps up against the Walmart World of Bentonville, making that corner of the Natural State the fastest growing and most affluent segment of a state that in most people's minds doesn't conjure up visions of growth and wealth. Of the towns that fill that stretch of I-49, none has seen more dramatic change and none is more diverse than Springdale. It was the perfect place for a little old lady, looking for anonymity, to find a buyer for gold dollars that bordered on being priceless.

Like most towns in Middle America, Springdale has seen its major retail businesses abandon the old town center for commercial strips along the highways. The Gold Standard, parent store to Mazatlán Numismatics, had resisted the move and remained entrenched on a quiet corner of Emma Avenue. Around it, a few small specialty shops and eateries survived, but much of the street now catered to the service sector: insurance brokers, attorneys, banks, and realtors.

I had awakened to an otherwise empty bed and emerged into the main living part of the house to an embarrassed and uneasy nod, offered amidst a flurry of breakfast preparation. Joseph continued her nervous scurry while I finished off a plate of bacon and eggs. She finally sat down to a bowl of raisin bran as I left to shower and dress. The drive into Arkansas was equally quiet, what little conversation we had concentrated on what I had tried to block from my mind the night before—what to say to the proprietor of The Gold Standard.

The young woman who greeted us across an L-shaped, counter looked to be in her early twenties, groomed and made-up in a way that made the most of an otherwise unremarkable face and figure. Her smile added to the appeal, and she hurried toward us as we entered the shop. Her pale face flushed brightly when I asked if she was the store manager.

"Not yet. That would be my father. Let me get him for you." She returned to the rear of the shop where a raised platform behind the back arm of the display counter was separated from the rest of the store by a paneled half-wall, accessed by three carpeted steps. She climbed to the platform before speaking quietly to some hidden figure. Good store manners, I thought. No shouting across the shop, even when we were the only patrons.

The man who appeared was as dark as the girl was pale. Thick as an angus bull with the hands and arms of a pro wrestler. But his features, balding head, and a less-myopic version of the wire-rimmed glasses we had seen on Rufus Pogue, showed him to be the man's son. A jeweler's magnifying lens was pushed up out of the way of his right eye.

"Thank you, Angela. And good morning." The voice was so soft and buttery that I would have sworn it couldn't be coming from this fullback of a man.

Joseph and I walked together toward the back counter. "Good morning," I said for both of us. "Can we speak privately somewhere for a few minutes?"

The younger Mr. Pogue glanced about the shop with an amused grin. "Looks pretty private to me right here. If someone comes in, Angela can help them, and we can slip up into the back." He held out a meaty hand. "David Pogue."

I looked cautiously at the girl as I shook his hand. "I mean 'very privately,' Mr. Pogue."

"Anything I can hear, she can hear," the big man said. "I'm training Angie to take over the store. There's no transaction too private for her to know about."

I gave a conceding nod and Joseph and I both held out our badges. "As you can see," Joseph began, "we're both Missouri law enforcement officers and have no jurisdiction here. But we're investigating a murder that you may be able to help us with. We would just as soon talk to you about it unofficially without all the hoopla it will take to bring in local authorities."

The jeweler smiled thinly and waved us to two stools that fronted the counter on our side, pulling another pair up across from us. He looked carefully from me to Joseph. "You're the couple who stopped in on my dad in Mazatlán. He thought you might be coming by here. Said you seemed more interested in where the Confederate dollars had come from than how much they might be worth." Young Pogue sat, but still seemed to fill all the space on the far side of the counter. Angela slipped behind one of the massive shoulders.

"We weren't entirely forthcoming with your father," I confessed, sliding onto one of the stools next to Joseph. "We're investigating the death of a woman named Nettie Suskey. One of the puzzles we've been trying to solve is how the woman supported herself. During a search of a safe deposit box, we found that she owned several coins that looked like genuine '61-Ds. Our follow-up investigation found the only recent sales to be from your shop in Mazatlán where we learned, much to our surprise, that they had come from a source not too far from Nettie's home. This shop. The Gold Standard."

At the mention of Nettie's name, David Pogue's brow had knitted almost unperceptively, but Angela's face had tightened and her eyes fluttered to blink back tears.

"Nettie brought her coins here, didn't she," Joseph said softly, directing her comment to the girl. Angela turned toward the big man who continued to look at us unflinchingly across the glass counter, then burst into tears and rushed up the stairs onto the back balcony. Her footsteps descended steps somewhere farther back and a door slammed.

Joseph kept her voice soft and even. "Do you want to tell us about that, Mr. Pogue?"

The thick chest rose with a long, nasal breath, then collapsed with a massive sigh. "Yes. Nettie's been coming here for a number of years. Brings one coin a year. We didn't even know her last name until now—or where she came from."

"That information wasn't important to a transaction of that size?" I questioned. "All cash with new hundred dollar bills and no last names? You must have given her tens of thousands of dollars for each coin. Do you have that kind of cash lying about just in case an old lady drops in with a priceless gold dollar?"

Pogue's dark eyes fixed a smoldering glare on mine. "We were always very fair with Nettie. The first time she came, we explained what we thought her coin would bring in an open sale and offered her two-thirds of that value. She insisted on half. Said she didn't need all that money and wouldn't know where to put it." He glanced back over his shoulder, then down through the glass of the countertop.

"She came down once or twice a year other than the purchase times. During those visits, she'd tell us when she would bring a coin. She and Angie got to be pretty close." He looked up at Joseph and smiled more broadly. "You probably couldn't tell, but Angela isn't my biological daughter. We worked with her through CASA, then had her as a foster kid for two years. Finally managed to talk the white court into letting us adopt her. Nettie was like a grandmother to her. What happened to her?"

"Someone broke into her home, ransacked the place, and smothered her."

David Pogue's eyes misted and he shook his head slowly. "Who could have done something like that to an old lady?"

Joseph waited while he blinked his eyes clear, then pressed, "She never told the girl her last name or where she lived?"

"Didn't seem to matter to either of them. Both saw themselves as people without much of a past worth remembering."

My turn for a question. "And you didn't need that personal information for financial reports?"

Pogue sat back and folded the trunks of his arms across his chest. "You got us there, I guess. You've been to Mexico. We don't sell the coins out of that store so we can keep close track of financial details. And we aren't in the Sinaloa province because we're looking for close Mexican oversight."

I wanted to suggest to Joseph that this might be a good time for us to step outside for a quick conference. But she seemed to be giving me her silent permission to be unprofessional and ignore Pogue's clear suggestion that they were skirting the law. "We're here to try to get answers to what happened to Nettie,"

I said. "We'll worry about the sales transaction if that appears to be a factor."

We heard the door open back on the balcony and could hear Angela scrape a chair closer to the half-wall.

"When did this happen?" Pogue asked.

Joseph answered. "Just over a week ago. We're looking for reasons. Someone knowing she had a supply of 1861-Ds seems like it could be one."

Pogue nodded. "Yup. That would be. We knew she had more than she'd brought down. But there was some real advantage to us in them coming to us one at a time and spread out." His dark face twisted into a cynical smile. "Scarcity adds value, and you always like to create the impression that the one up for auction might be the last."

"How many did she say she had?"

His shrug absorbed what little we could see of his thick neck. "She was here a few months ago. We knew from what she said that there were a few more."

I stepped back in. "What did she say that led you to believe that?"

He had also heard Angela return and called to her over his shoulder. "Angie? Why don't you come on back down here. You can help me with this."

She appeared at the steps, pink-faced and puffy-eyed. This time Pogue had her sit on the stool beside him. "Do you know anything about CASA?" he asked.

Joseph looked blank, so I answered. "We have a small chapter in the county. Court Appointed Special Advocates. Volunteers who work with kids in foster care so they have someone who's keeping an eye out for them while they're in the foster system."

Joseph was free with her ignorance. "Don't all foster kids have a social worker assigned?"

Angela sniffed. "To you and maybe fifty others. And that's

a real burnout job. I had four or five during the years I was in foster care."

"And how many of these CASA volunteers?" Joseph asked.

Angela turned to the giant beside her and her eyes again misted. "Only one. Mom and Dad."

Mr. Pogue wrapped a burly arm about his daughter. "Nettie was quite taken with the whole CASA idea," he said. "She knew there was a chapter where she lived and that foster numbers were growing. When she was here last, she even told us she was planning to change her will to leave the rest of her coins to her local CASA group. That's how I knew there were more."

While Joseph was learning about Court Appointed Special Advocates, I had been looking over a 1907 twenty-dollar gold piece in the case below my elbows. My eyes snapped back to the big black man at mention of Nettie's will. "She talked about changing her will?"

He gave a smooth, honey-coated chuckle. "Yes. She'd been thinking about it for months, but was afraid to tell some friend of hers that she was being shut out."

"Some friend who'd been told she was in the will?"

Pogue nodded. "That's the way I understood it. Nettie wanted to have her will redone to give everything to CASA."

Joseph had also shifted her attention to the jeweler. "Did she name this friend?"

"No. She never really talked about having any good friends, did she, Angela? But this was someone she'd written into her will." Angela shook her head, still dabbing at her eyes with a Kleenex.

I looked over at Joseph and saw that she agreed it was time to wrap this one up. I pushed my stool back and stood, reaching across the glass to place a consoling hand on the girl's. "Sorry we had to be the bearers of bad news. I know Nettie must have appreciated your friendship and . . ." I shot Pogue a knowing grin. ". . . and your business assistance. Thanks for being so helpful." I dropped a card onto the glass top and Joseph did the same. "If you think of anything else that might be useful to us, give me a call. We're not that far away."

David Pogue picked up the card, flipped it over for a quick look at the empty back, then ran his eyes over the front. "Crayton, Missouri," he muttered. "That's where Nettie was from?"

"Near there. Out in the country."

"That's *not* too far," he said.

"No," I acknowledged, watching the merchant's eyes. "A man could be there in just over an hour."

His lids drooped thoughtfully, his eyes dropping again to the counter. "Have they had her services yet? Angie and her mother and I would like to come up."

"Nothing arranged yet," I said. "But if you'll give me a card, I'll send details when we get them."

He picked a gold-embossed card from a holder on the counter. "Please do. She was very good to us."

That, I thought, was something of an understatement.

25

Nothing was said until we were on Highway 62 headed north along the west side of Beaver Lake. That seemed to have become our habit: spend some time thinking after each interview, then talk it through. But it wasn't Angela or David Pogue that Joseph had on her mind.

"We messed up, Tate," she said before I could raise the question of the will.

"You mean by not pushing Brenda Castoe harder about the will?"

"No. By sleeping together."

"Oh." I'd been thinking about it off and on all day, but not as a topic of conversation for the drive home. I was thinking more of asking her to stay over again tonight. "You're having some regrets?"

"It was nice, Tate. Very nice. But I promised I wouldn't mix business and pleasure again. And I screwed up, so to speak. It was a mistake."

"I thought it was wonderful. I was going to ask you to stay again tonight."

"See? That's what I mean. Another night or two, and we'll be thinking we need to drive back and forth between our places and start something regular. I'm not ready for that."

I drove a few miles without saying anything, unsure what to say and less sure how to say whatever I finally decided on. When I couldn't see a car in front or behind, giving me some made-no-sense feeling of privacy, I said, "I'm not sure I'd find that a bad thing. I haven't really cared for anyone for a long time, and I do care for you. Is that a bad thing?"

"Yes," she said emphatically. "It's a bad thing. I haven't cared for anyone in any serious way for a long time either. I'm feeling like another night or two in your company and that will be over. I can't have that."

"If it's happening, why not let it happen?"

"Oh, how do I answer that? Let me count the ways." She gazed out the window for her own few miles of silence, then said, "First of all, when you start caring too much about a partner, you act differently. And react differently. That's not always safe in law enforcement. Like when we went down after the Greaves. We needed to be thinking about procedure, not about the other's safety all the time."

"I think we'd have done pretty much the same thing. We're always covering the other's back."

"Yes. But not always rushing in to take the first shots so the other doesn't get it. That's what I mean."

"I don't think either of us rushed in on the Greaves to keep the other from doing it."

"Okay. Bad example. But you know what I mean. We can't let our feelings about each other color our professional judgment."

I gave that a thoughtful nod. "But how I feel about you isn't going to change if we're not sleeping together. I'll be worrying about you just the same way."

"Not true," she said with the same certainty with which she had started this conversation. "It makes a *big* difference. There's this . . ." She struggled for the word. ". . . this *intimacy* that develops that changes things."

"Like, what does it change?" I asked, partly to be argumentative and partly because I wanted to know.

"*I swear*," she snapped back, turning again to the window. "You dicks-for-brains men! Don't you have *any* feelings of affection that don't end with an ejaculation?"

"Hey, now," I defended. "I told you I was getting pretty into you way before I really got into you. And if I'm remembering right, I was all snuggled in and having a pretty good sleep when you slipped in beside me and grabbed me from behind."

"You said you'd been hoping I'd come. And I could tell you had."

"Okay. So I was hoping. But you were the one who came to my room."

"Well, it can't happen again. For another thing, I'm waiting to get transferred back to St. Louis as soon as there's an opening. I don't want to spend the rest of my career driving about in these hills worrying I might have just rolled in poison ivy."

"You didn't get poison ivy. Instead, you got a trip to Mexico. You'd give that up to go work in the city?"

"In a heartbeat."

She was beginning to piss me off. "Well, when we get back to our outpost of civilization, you can just motor on up to Springfield and get your papers in for a transfer."

"They've been in for a long time," she said glumly. "And I owe it to you to see this case through." Before I could say, "You don't owe me anything," she continued, "So—what about Pogue's saying Brenda Castoe knew about the will?"

My mind was still processing the possibility of Joseph being transferred back to St. Louis and how I'd feel about it. It took me a few seconds to shift gears. When back in low, I asked, "What makes you think it was Brenda she was talking about?"

Joseph seemed to have left "No sleeping together" and "Transfer to St. Louis" miles behind.

"Who else would it be?" She glanced over as if that whole last twenty minutes hadn't happened. "We know she's in the will we've seen and she denied knowing about it."

"Right. But if Nettie had been inclined to change the thing, wouldn't she have gone ahead and changed it after the CASA discussion."

163

"In just the last few weeks? No. She was still trying to get the nerve up to tell Brenda."

"Or she told her, then didn't have a chance to get the will changed."

"Yes. Or that," Joseph agreed. "In fact, I'm kind of leaning in that direction."

"What about Angela and David Pogue? They certainly had a vested interest. And that guy could pin an old lady in a chair and hardly know she was there."

"Did they seem like killers to you? The girl loved the old lady and, as David said, they benefited from having a new coin show up once a year. Since they didn't know where she lived, they wouldn't know about the valley being flooded and Nettie having to move."

"*If* they didn't know where she lived. And if they had all the coins, they could still dole them out once a year."

"We need to see if Pogue Junior has prints on record that we can run against our mystery set."

I carefully lifted the gold embossed card from my pocket. "I'd guess we have a pretty good thumb, index, and middle finger right here."

26

We made it to the office without another mention of the night before. Grace met us when we walked in, gave Joseph a quick full-body scan that said to me "Why does she get to wear those jeans that make her butt look so good instead of patrol uniform pants?" I wanted to remind her that she *chose* to wear uniform pants precisely, I believed, because she thought they made *her* figure look better. In fact, was there something different about her today? Something that made her even prettier? Maybe my growing attraction to Joseph was freeing my shackled interest in women since Adeena's death to be more appreciative in general. Grace interrupted my thoughts.

"Galen Suskey's waiting in your office." She pushed past us to the side table that held the coffee machine and poured herself a cup, not looking back again at either of us.

I checked my mail basket in the rack by the door and thumbed through to see if anything looked urgent. Nothing did. "Did he say what he wants?"

Grace swung back past us toward her desk, confirming my suspicion that something was different. A touch of vanilla? And had she decided to wear a little makeup?

"He wants to know where you are on the case. I guess he's been pushing Judge Werner for some decision on who the property goes to. His Honor said he's not hearing any claims or deciding anything until you finish your investigation."

I glanced back at Joseph who was pouring her own cup of coffee. "You want to sit in on this?"

Grace shot a quick look over her shoulder to see if I was speaking to her, plopped the cup hard enough on her desk to splash a black stream onto the blotter, and dropped heavily into her chair.

"I was directing that to both of you," I said, dancing a little two-step toward my office door. Grace didn't lift her eyes. "I think you may want me with you," she muttered, swiping at the spill with a wad of tissue. "I've been following up on the man's whereabouts at the time of the murder and his story doesn't exactly jive with what I've learned."

"Both of you, then. Marti, could you help Grace with her spill?" Marti had been watching our little office drama with silent amusement. She nodded and headed toward the paper towel dispenser in the office restroom. Grace tossed the soaked Kleenex into her wastebasket and led into the office with Joseph trailing.

The Galen Suskey who sat in the chair facing mine across the desk was not the same Galen who had been dangling his feet above the floor a week before. It was the same squat, paunchy frame. But this man's gray hair was neatly trimmed into a conservative cut above his ears and his face was clean shaven. His stumpy body was wrapped in clean faded jeans and a new off-the-rack navy sports jacket that looked a size too small for his soft stomach. He didn't stand as we came in, but glanced quickly over at Grace as she moved to a folding chair in the corner, then gave Joseph a long nervous stare.

"I just come to talk to *you*," he grumbled before I'd reached my side of the desk. Joseph settled into the armchair beside the window, leaning back comfortably with arms folded.

"Officer Joseph is with the State Patrol," I said. "She's one of the investigators on Nettie's case. Officer Torres you've met. She's been doing some follow-up work that might be important to our discussion."

Galen Suskey shifted slightly to give Joseph another long look. "The State Police is working on this too?"

"We're a small office here and don't have some of the

resources the state has. We want to give Nettie's case all the professional attention we can. Officer Joseph is one of their best."

"*Humph,*" Suskey grunted. "So what you finding out?"

"I'm not free to share all of the details, but we're making good progress. Is there something specific I can help you with?"

The man shifted nervously in the chair, leaning forward with elbows on his knees. "I been to see the judge. Like I told you before, there never was no will nor nothin' that gave that land to Nettie. It was as much mine as hers. I knew we couldn't make a living off the land, so I went off to work while Nettie kept the place up. Seems like now it should just be comin' to me. But the judge says he won't be decidin' what happens to it 'til you get this case figured out. I was hopin' maybe you could let him know I'm in the clear on this, so should be able to get title to the land before it all gets covered over."

Grace answered from her corner. "Where have you been the last few weeks, Mr. Suskey?"

He refused to make the effort to swing around toward her, keeping his eyes on me. "What do you mean, where have I been? And what's that got to do with anything?"

"What I mean is that I checked with your landlady in Nowata. She says you moved out almost a month ago. Where have you been the last three weeks?"

"I been just kickin' around. My next month's rent was comin' up and I was planning on comin' over here to check on the property anyway. I knew it was bein' flooded."

"But you didn't come right away."

"I had some other stuff I needed to do 'cause of my pension. Had to go back over to Bartlesville. I got here the day I come in to see you."

"I know you're staying out at the Super 8 on the highway and checked in that day. Can you tell me where you were staying in Bartlesville?"

"Stayin' with a friend of mine from the oil days."

"I'll need a name and address on this friend," Grace said evenly.

"Name's Calvin Latty. Don't know his address. Creek Street or Creek Avenue. I just know how to get there. I'll have to call him."

"When we're through here. But speaking of friends, I've been checking around to see who you might know that would be keeping you posted on what's going on in town. There aren't many people left who remember that far back. But those who do, said you really only hung out with one person. Who do you think they said that was, Mr. Suskey?"

The little man's jaw tightened beneath the wattle of his chin. "You're the smart police lady. You tell me."

Grace's expression didn't change. "The neighbor kid at the next place down in Blackjack Holler. LJ Greaves. I hear that until you left for the oil fields, LJ was about the only friend you had."

I glanced over at Joseph who was working as hard as I was not to show surprise. She jumped into what was rapidly becoming an interrogation.

"LJ Greaves been keeping you up on what's going on here, Mr. Suskey?"

He shifted just enough to straighten toward me, but stopped there. "So, what if he has? His place is bein' flooded too. But I ain't heard nothing from him since you shot him."

I'd been taking this all in, wondering about our visitor's new clothes and haircut, when a light went off in my head that should have been switched on long ago. Another rookie oversight. "Was it you who told the Greaves they could cut timber on the family property?"

Suskey's eyes narrowed. "Hell, yes, it was me. I have as much right to what goes on there as anyone. So what if it was me?"

"And they gave you shares of what they got for the logs?"

"Damn right, they did."

"But none to Nettie."

Galen Suskey's shoulders rolled nervously to force a kink from his hunched back. "I figured Nettie was getting her share of the place through the buyout. Didn't know if any of that would come to me. So I figured I'd get what I could while I could."

"And when Nettie found out about this, the Greaves killed her," Grace suggested coldly.

This time Suskey swung abruptly toward her. "Hell, no. She had no idea they was cutting back there. I told 'em to stay on the back forty and she couldn't tell they wasn't on their place. She wasn't gettin' anything done with the timber and it was all going to go underwater. She'd a never knowed."

Joseph spoke from her side of the room, bringing Suskey's attention back to center. I was beginning to feel a little sorry about the way we were torqueing his stumpy frame from side-to-side. "Maybe she *did* find out and threatened to report them," Joseph continued. "I can see them doing your sister in if they thought she was going to report them."

Suskey rolled his head nervously from side-to-side, swinging the wattle like a bulging udder. "LJ called when you found her dead. He was as surprised as anyone. I'd told them they could cut but better stop. I figured the law would come snoopin' around. But I said if you did, all he needed to do was push that off on me."

"You say he called?" Joseph questioned. "How did he get to you if you'd moved?"

Suskey threw his weight back in the chair and fished a phone from his pocket. "We both got cells." He held up an aging iPhone. "He'd check in every week to let me know what was goin' on."

I reached across the desk. "I'd like you to leave your phone, please, Mr. Suskey. I know you don't have to without a warrant, but I'd just as soon not have to march you across the street to the judge to get one, especially if you're working on making a good impression on him."

His face folded into a creased frown. "You makin' me a suspect? Hell, your deputy woman over there can check to see that I was in Bartlesville. I was goin' into the union office every day. Give 'em a call."

"We will," I assured him. "But right now, everyone's being looked at, and I need your phone." I slid a pad of post-it notes across in front of him. "If you have a password, please write it down. And include the name of the friend you were staying with in Oklahoma, and his address and number."

Suskey laid the phone on the desktop and scribbled on the pad. "I'll be wantin' this back," he growled. "And you ain't goin' to find nothing on there but calls to LJ. Maybe a call or two to Calvin."

"Did you ever call Verl?" Joseph asked. Suskey didn't look up, but I saw his brow furrow. "Don't know that I did. And before you ask, no. I don't know where Verl is." He finished writing, pushed off the arms of the chair to vault forward onto the floor, and faced me across the desk. "You got anything else to ask me?"

I glanced at my partners who both gave me a quick shake of the head. Grace headed toward the door to open it for him. "Doesn't look like it, Mr. Suskey," I said. "But you need to stay in town. Nothing creates suspicion more than someone trying to disappear when they're on the list."

"I'm waitin' to claim my property. That's what I come in here for in the first place." He glared over at Grace. "You know I'm at the Super 8, room 115." He pushed the chair aside and slouched past Grace and out into the main office. She pushed the door quietly closed behind him.

We sat for our customary silent moment, looking around at each other. Before either of the others could lead us in a different direction, I spoke to Grace who was leaning, arms folded, against the door frame.

"There were a couple of little surprises from you in the questions you asked Suskey. When did you plan to share the information about him leaving his place in Oklahoma a month ago, and being close to LJ Greaves?"

Her eyes narrowed, but she didn't budge. "When you were in here long enough to learn what the rest of us have been doing. And I just learned some of that this morning."

"It's the kind of thing you always call about as soon as you learn it."

"I think that was when you weren't spending most of your time in Mexico, or Springdale, or Springfield."

I was tempted to snap back but didn't want more said about Mexico. Instead, I asked, "So, what do you think after this little interview?"

"I'm thinking we need to get into that phone, see who he's called and when, and maybe find a number that can lead us to Verl. And that I need to call this 'friend' in Bartlesville and check out his story."

I grunted agreement and turned to Joseph who was watching our exchange with a tight smile. "And Officer Joseph, what are you thinking?"

She leaned back and linked her hands behind her head. "As Mr. Suskey talked, I was thinking that each day—in fact, more often than that—I've had a new name at the top of my list. This morning I was suspecting the coin merchants. Seemed nice and helpful, but had a huge interest in keeping Nettie's money coming their way. Then, when I learned Nettie was thinking of changing her will and that Brenda Castoe may have lied to us about knowing she was in it, my suspicions shifted to her. But if Mr. Suskey was working with the Greaves on stripping the timber from the property without Nettie knowing, that's a pretty damning motive."

Grace had relaxed more completely against the door frame but straightened and glared at me with her dark, Latin eyes as Joseph spoke.

"So you learned that Brenda Castoe knew she was in the will and lied about it?" she snapped. "That's the kind of thing we usually call each other about. I could have been in Springfield this morning asking her about it."

I nodded to concede that communication had been lax on both sides. "As you said, we've all had too many things going on. We both need to do better from now on." I pushed from the chair, signaling Joseph to come with me. "Grace, go through this phone with a fine-toothed comb. We need to know who every call went to. And we need a good time profile of the calls. Then check on the friend in Bartlesville and call the union office."

She continued to prop up the door frame. "And you two? What will you be up to?"

"I think we both need to talk to Brenda," I called back to her as we headed for the outer door. "Then I want to get over to Cox Medical and see if LJ is in any shape to talk."

27

Marti caught me on the way out of the office with a list of the things that had come up during the morning. The school district wondered if I could sit in on two parent-teacher conferences with Syrian families who had been taken in by the First Christian Church and needed interpreting help.

"Next Tuesday afternoon about 3:30," she read from the note. "That's what you get for being the only person within fifty miles who speaks both English and Arabic."

"Something I like to help with," I agreed. "Put me down and note it on my calendar. Anything more criminal?"

"Somebody stole seven of the Collins' calves. Backed a trailer up to one of their gates last night and herded them in."

I chuckled, then assured Marti when she responded with a withering glare, "No one from around here. And pretty stupid of them. First of all, no one from the county would mess with one of the commissioners' stock. And anyone who knows cattle wouldn't steal calves from Collins. He's cross-bred his Charolais this year with Angus bulls and got a litter of pretty unique-looking gray calves. When they try to unload them, it'll be like trying to sell a '37 Rolls Phantom at the local auto auction."

Marti shook her head. "Why would anybody take them then? Frankie went out when we got the call and got the details. But I'd guess Bob will be expecting to hear from you. The commissioners usually want the head man."

"I'll call him on my way to Springfield. Did Frankie find tire tracks?"

"Yes. And made casts. This was his kind of call. We've got fifty pounds of plaster and about a dozen print sets in the evidence room."

"And he's called the sale barns around? Asked them to

watch for a load of gray calves?"

"Yes. That's been done."

"Ask him to call all the meat lockers that butcher beef. And contact trailer rentals in the area. See who's rented stock trailers in the last few days. Go as far out as Springfield, down into Arkansas, and over into the corner of Kansas. If he finds one that would haul seven calves, let's get tire prints on it. And get a number for Sheriff Parnell over in Montgomery County, Kansas."

Marti jotted a note to herself and went to an old rolodex file she kept on the corner of her desk. "You think these people came from that far away?"

"They didn't know cattle and didn't know our county. I'm guessing they want money, not cows. They won't try the sale barns because they don't know how they work. So I'm guessing a rented trailer and an attempt to sell them to a meat locker or feed lot. Those calves are pretty young for slaughter, so I'd put my money on the KAMO feedlot over in Sheriff Parnell's county. It's notorious for not asking questions."

Marti flipped through the file and found Parnell's number. "I'll send it to your phone so you have it," she suggested. "And Bob Collins' number too."

I repeated the chuckle and this time she grinned back. "Oh, right," she said. "His would already be on your speed dial."

"From the day the commissioners hired me," I assured her. "Anything else need attention before I head north?"

"That's it for now. And Rocky should be back in the next half hour. I heard you give Grace her marching orders. If anything else comes up, Rocky can handle it."

I called Bob Collins as I drove, gave him a rundown on what we were doing to find his stock, then checked in with Joseph who was half an hour ahead of me.

"I was able to track down Brenda Castoe," she began. "She didn't sound thrilled, but will meet with us at the Troop D offices on Kearney Street at 5:30. That should give us time to stop in on Mr. Greaves before we see her. Want to meet me at Cox Medical Center?"

"Send me a room number when you get there and wait," I suggested. "If you walk in by yourself, he may either clam up or have heart failure."

"I'll meet you in the lobby," she said.

LJ was only about half a heartbeat out of intensive care. We found him with liquid flowing into both arms and tubes and wires taped to most everything else. The nurse who gave us ten minutes with him cautioned that he might be hoarse and still sedated.

"He's had tubes in his nose and throat until this morning, so he may have trouble talking," she warned. "And he's still on a sedative. We weren't certain we'd save him for the first few days."

I glanced over at Joseph to see if she'd make any comment about her "do not resuscitate" request. She'd apparently put that behind her. "I didn't think the wound was that life-threatening," she said instead.

The nurse picked up his chart. "Rib fragments punctured and collapsed one of his lungs. And there was some kind of secondary infection. Anyway, like I said. No more than ten minutes."

LJ was conscious enough to follow us with his eyes as we circled to the window side of his partially-raised bed. I'd suggested on the way up that I do the questioning. The old man probably wasn't as likely to respond well to the woman who'd put him in intensive care.

"Or he might respond better," she argued. "Knows I'm not someone who's just bullshitting him."

"Let's start out my way on this one," I insisted. "If he doesn't budge, you can try yours."

LJ wasn't too committed to making things easy for either of us. When I asked how he was feeling, he croaked out what I understood to be a suggestion about what the two of us could do to each other. I plowed ahead anyway.

"I need to ask you a few questions about Nettie Suskey's death. Why didn't you tell us Galen Suskey had given you permission to cut trees?"

LJ's eyes flitted from me to Joseph and back. "I don't remember you givin' us time to tell you anything," he growled. "The bitch shot me before we could say nothin'."

"You had plenty of time before she showed up. When I was asking about cutting trees."

"Wasn't none of your business."

"With Nettie having been killed? Did she find you back there? Or did you go tell her, and she said Galen didn't have any right to be letting you cut? Which was it, LJ?"

The man's sunken eyes again shifted between us. Joseph's face was a stone mask. He took a deep swallow. "You must have talked to Galen. So what did he tell you?"

"Galen was pretty nervous about it. I think he's worried that one of you did it."

His eyes narrowed. He reached out a tethered hand and tipped ice chips into his mouth from a plastic cup, sucking at them for a few moments before answering. "He told you that? I don't think so. Galen wouldn't turn on us like that. He believed Verl when he came back from the house."

Joseph stepped closer to the bed. "When Verl came back from Nettie's house?" LJ looked at her quickly, then back to me. "We was talkin' by phone, me and Galen. He decided we should tell her, but didn't want to come to town yet. Verl got along with the old woman better than I did. She's always hated my guts. Wouldn't piss on me if I was on fire." He gulped some more ice, sucked at it, then added, "She always thought I steered Galen wrong. Been a *bad influence* on him. So Verl went over."

"And she didn't like what she heard, so he killed her," Joseph finished for him.

"You stay out of this, bitch," he snarled without looking at her. "I'll be havin' my lawyer come talk to you. Verl came back and said he'd found her dead. Said the place smelled like hell, and he stuck his head in to see what was goin' on. She was dead in her chair."

Joseph started to say something and I gave her arm a quieting squeeze. "We checked for prints in the room and didn't find Verl's, LJ. Why would he have been worried about leaving prints if he was just going to talk to her?"

LJ snorted painfully. "Sometimes you law people can be such dumb asses. We were cutting logs when Galen called to say he thought we'd better tell her. Verl wears them leather gloves like a second skin when he's workin,. Wouldn't have taken them off."

I couldn't restrain Joseph. "Very convenient," she muttered. "You're poaching her trees, Verl goes to tell her, and comes back to say he found her dead. And you didn't let anybody know?"

"We called Galen," LJ rasped. "Told him. Then we all decided we'd be better off to let someone else find her. Otherwise, you'd be thinkin' just what you're thinkin'."

The nurse stepped into the room, holding up her wrist to show an Apple watch. "Time," she said. "In fact, I've given you more than I should. You need to let Mr. Greaves get some rest."

I needed time to think on what he'd just told us anyway, so her timing was good. I just had one final question. "Where's Verl?" I asked as the nurse put her hand on my elbow to turn me toward the door. "We need to talk to him about this."

"No idea," he croaked after us. "If he wants to talk to you, he'll come find you."

As we exited into the hall, I asked the nurse what I had intended to when we first came up, but she'd gotten away too quickly. "Where's the security for this man? He turned a weapon on a police officer and has charges against him."

She gave me one of those "I put up with you people because I have to" frowns. "You saw the man. He couldn't walk to the nursing station without help. When he becomes ambulatory, we'll have someone watch him. And by the way," she said, deciding to be more helpful. "I heard your last question. Someone's been calling his room phone to check on him two or three times a day. A man. You might check with our admin downstairs for the incoming number."

I gave her a nod and followed Joseph into the elevator.

"Who's calling?" she wondered. "Galen or Verl?"

"I'd put my money on Verl. I think Galen wants to keep what distance he can from his old pal right now."

"Verl calling to see if he's getting better? Or hoping he isn't?"

"Or maybe to find out if anyone's come to talk to him. See what he'd said."

Joseph nodded. "If it's a cell phone, it may show us where he is. Do you think he killed her?"

"One thing troubles me," I wondered aloud as the elevator door slid open on the main floor. "Telling LJ that the place smelled like hell when he came back seems like a strange thing to say if he killed her while he was there. I'd think he'd just say he found her dead. He couldn't be sure LJ might want to go back over there or call it into my office."

"Or LJ could be lying about the whole thing," she suggested.

He could, I thought, but the old man had been slurring what he said just enough to sound half-sedated. I doubted he was thinking clearly enough to lie.

"Let's see if we can get that phone number. I'll call Grace and ask her to trace the location of the calls while we talk to Brenda. I don't see our emergency alert lady as being in the clear yet."

Joseph led me to the board that listed hospital offices. "That's the problem," she muttered. "I don't think anybody's in the clear yet."

28

Hospitals are obsessive about records of any kind, even if they don't seem at all related to health issues. The administrative assistant called her boss who said she would at least look up the calls to LJ's room and have an incoming number available to us if we could get a subpoena. Joseph called the office of her judge friend and we headed up toward Kearney to the Troop D headquarters.

Brenda Castoe paced the floor of the reception area like a caged lioness, dressed as she always was in a calf-length dress and sensible shoes. She showed none of the chipper helpfulness we had seen when she first met us at the Grillhouse.

"I hope this isn't going to become a regular thing," she complained as we entered the building. "I had to cancel an afternoon appointment that I've now had to slide for another two weeks."

We had agreed that Joseph would be lead on this interview. She had called ahead to schedule a room and the receptionist handed her a note as we entered.

"We think we're getting close to wrapping this case up," she said to Brenda, leading us into the back of the building to a small conference room. "You offered to help in any way you can, and there are a few things you can clear up for us." Joseph pulled out the chair nearest the door, invited Brenda to sit, and walked around the table to sit opposite her. I took a seat at the end of the table, leaving the conversation to the women.

Brenda sat with hands folded primly in front of her, chin lifted and eyes set on Joseph. "Am I still a suspect in this case?" she demanded.

"We are gradually eliminating suspects," Joseph said evenly. "That's why we wanted to meet with you this afternoon. We have some new information we think you can clarify for us." Brenda's jaw clenched resolutely, but she blinked nervously across at her interrogator. She said nothing about doing all she could to help.

"When we met last," Joseph began, "we informed you that you have been named in Nettie Suskey's will as her sole heir. You seemed surprised at that, and insisted you had no idea she was leaving what she had to you."

"I didn't," Brenda insisted.

Joseph's expression remained impassive. "We have been told since, by a very credible source, that Nettie had informed you of her intentions to make you her heir."

The woman started to protest, paused in what appeared to be genuine confusion, then slumped slightly forward. "I didn't think she was being serious," she whispered into the table. "Quite a long time ago, maybe two years, she told me I was about the only person who seemed to care at all about her. She said she might just have to leave everything she had to me."

"And you didn't believe she meant it?" Joseph pressed.

Brenda lifted her chin and looked glumly across at Joseph. "What was there to believe? The woman had nothing. At the time she was having one of her bouts of depression. I just thought she was trying to find some way to thank me for being kind. I didn't see it as a serious thing."

"So you wouldn't have taken it any more seriously if she later told you she was leaving what she had to someone else?"

Brenda smiled thinly. "I would have thought the same thing. That there was nothing to give away, and she was just having another depression episode. They were pretty regular."

"And you never seriously wondered how the woman supported herself? When we talked last, you said you knew she had some source of income, but chose not to ask about it."

"I also told you," the woman said indignantly, "that our company policies are very clear about avoiding financial discussions with our clients. We want there to be no suggestion that we are doing anything to take advantage of them."

"And we told you during our last meeting that Nettie had a small fortune in property. You must have known that."

Brenda's indignation grew. "I can see that I'm still under suspicion. I think it may not be wise for me to say more about my work with Nettie without talking to my company people and maybe getting legal advice."

"Do you need legal advice, Brenda?" Joseph asked.

"I need to quit being hauled in every week to be harassed by you people." Her voice was now razor-sharp. "And if you're through with this little interrogation, I have things to do." She stood abruptly and glared across at Joseph. "But I will tell you one thing. I had no idea how much property Nettie Suskey had before you told me. As far as I knew, she lived on a little patch of land down in that valley, and those good-for-nothing men behind her she was always complaining about owned right up to the back of her trailer. Now. Can I go?"

Joseph looked over at me and I nodded. "Yes, you can go," Joseph said. "But as we told you before, stay around town until this is all resolved."

"Why would I go anywhere else?" Brenda snapped back at her and tromped out of the office, her sensible shoes clicking hard against the tile floor as she left the building.

We had our moment of silence. "Like I said before," Joseph said finally, "she's either telling us the truth or is a very talented actress. Which way do you lean?"

I pushed up out of the chair and stood with hands flat against the tabletop. "Sometimes I feel like a real asshole having to pressure people like that. You did it well. Is she lying? I hope not. She seems like one of the more decent people involved in this whole mess."

"Seemingly decent people do terrible things sometimes," Joseph reminded me. "The Pogues seem decent. I'd hate that Angela to be involved. We'd better be hoping for the Greaves if we don't want decent." Her phone rattled against the tabletop. She answered, listened in silence, then thanked the caller.

"Our judge got a subpoena delivered right to the hospital," she announced. "They not only got the incoming number from their phone service but managed to get a point of origin. All the calls came through a tower in Muskogee, Oklahoma."

Joseph insisted that her need to stay in Springfield for a few days and get caught up on other work had nothing to do with not wishing to spend another night in close proximity to yours truly.

"See if you can track down Verl," she said as she pushed open the door of her own office at Troop D headquarters. "And call when we have something that needs both of our attention."

"I'll need someone to go to Muskogee with me," I protested. "If I find Verl, I don't want to try to deal with him by myself."

Joseph looked back with a wry grin. "Take that chief deputy along. She's been angling for more of your time." She reached over and squeezed my hand. "Call me when you have something," and disappeared into her office.

I called Grace from the parking lot and told her about Muskogee.

"No surprise here," she said. "I managed to get into Galen Suskey's phone and two of the most recent calls were to a motel in Muskogee. The America's Best Value Inn."

"The password Galen gave us was right?"

Grace chuckled. "He didn't strike me as a guy who was very tech savvy, or one who wanted to try to remember a complicated password. Did you look at what he wrote down? 4567. And that was it."

"Have you called the motel?"

"Not yet. I wanted to talk to you first. If Verl's there, I don't want to do anything to spook him."

"Good thinking. Anything else on the phone that helps?"

"Lots of calls to and from a phone I'd guess is LJ's. One of them early the morning you found Nettie. Nothing recently."

"Before we found her?"

"Yeah. More than an hour before."

I *humphed* into the phone. "That pretty well jives with the story we got from the old man this morning. He said Verl went over to tell Nettie her brother had given them permission to cut timber and found her dead. Went back, and LJ called Galen. They decided they'd better stay quiet about it and let someone else find the body."

"Or he went over to see if anyone had discovered it yet," Grace suggested. "They may have called Galen to tell him to stay away a little longer."

I started up the Explorer and headed her way. "Always that possibility," I agreed. "We need to talk to Verl. Call the Muskogee police and ask them to send someone over to the

Best Value Inn. Get them his mug shot. If he's there, have them pick him up and hold him 'til we get there on a charge of attempted murder." I paused, then added, "Ask them to check his room and pickup for a Marlin 336."

"You headed directly over there?"

"No. I'm coming by to get you. Tell Marti to find Rocky and Frankie and have them where she can get in touch with them if calls come in."

"The state investigator isn't free to go along on this one?" Grace asked, unable to completely hide the sarcasm.

"I want you with me. This is our case, and I think Verl is key to it in some way."

Her tone softened. "I'll get the notice to the Muskogee PD. How far out are you?"

"Just leaving Springfield. I'll see you in about an hour-thirty."

"You want to drive over there tonight? That's at least three hours."

"Yes. Have Marti find us a place to stay. If they locate our man, I want to be right there."

"I'll go pick up a change of clothes. I guess you'll need to stop."

"No. I keep a change with me."

"Oh, yes. I guess you do." The edge was back in her voice.

29

We dropped down into Arkansas and crossed into Oklahoma on 412 through Siloam Springs. The GPS showed it would be faster to take I-44, but that meant going north before heading west, and that didn't seem right to me. I'd just as soon be heading in the direction we're supposed to be going, even if it takes a little longer.

We didn't get out of Crayton until almost 8:00. Grace had picked up a couple of sub sandwiches at Casey's on the highway and we both worked on an Italian combo while I drove. It gave us the catch-up time she said she'd been going without.

The rural roads were completely dark by the time we got into Arkansas, giving the inside of the patrol car a kind of intimacy that brought Grace closer than any time we'd spent together. It made both of us a little uneasy. We ate without talking until most of my sandwich was gone. I was fishing in the Casey's bag for an apple fritter when she broke the silence.

"Galen was in Bartlesville with this Calvin Latty until the day before he showed up at the office. He had some pension issue he was straightening out and didn't leave until late the afternoon before he arrived in town. I talked to Latty and the union office people. They said he was there most of the day we know Nettie was killed. This Calvin says he can account for Suskey's time when he wasn't at the union shop. I think we can pretty safely say he wasn't our killer."

"Did you run anything on Calvin Latty?"

"I did. No criminal record and no prints under that name. The union people said he was one of their retired members."

I gave her the details of our conversation with LJ and my impression of Brenda Castoe's story.

She wrapped an unfinished half of her sandwich and slipped it back into the store bag, finishing off the last of her drink. "It sounds like you believe both," she said, reaching back over the seat to stow the sack.

"Talking to villagers in Iraq, I think I developed a pretty good sense for who was telling me the truth and who was setting me up or covering their ass," I said. "LJ seemed too drugged up to keep a lie straight. Brenda was more angry than scared."

"So what are you thinking?"

"I'm thinking I could be completely wrong. But both stories will hold up well unless someone gives us better information than we have now."

"And you're hoping to get that from Verl."

"Some of it. And what are *you* thinking?" I glanced over to try to measure her reaction. The glow from the dash lit her face in profile against the window and I couldn't escape the thought that she truly was a remarkably pretty woman. Deciding Mara Joseph was worth knowing better had definitely loosened the cloak of grief and self-pity I'd been wrapped in for the past two years, a cloak that had been covering Grace as much as me. *But I work with Grace*, I was reminding myself when she turned toward me, holding my eyes long enough that I suspected she knew what I was thinking.

"I've been keeping a suspect board in the office with the people who seem possibilities. Verl and LJ. Galen Suskey and Brenda Castoe. David Pogue in Springdale and possibly his daughter, though from what you told me, she seems unlikely."

"Old Mr. Pogue in Mazatlán," I added. "We need to keep him on the list for now. And his security man, Miguel."

She shook her head in the shadows of the car. "One other bit of information I forgot to relay to you in all of our not keeping each other informed. I checked with ICE on Pogue Senior. He hasn't been back in the country since he moved to Mexico. David and Angela go to see him about once a year but not since well before Nettie died. He never comes back to the States."

"So not old Mr. Pogue. That gives us six suspects or someone who's not even on our radar. A random robbery by the owner of the unidentified prints? Someone in the county who somehow got wind Nettie had a hidden fortune or money in the trailer?"

"I've had Rocky keeping his ear to the gossip hotline," Grace murmured from the dark. "He's pretty well connected to the druggies and good-for-nothings around. He generally hears when someone's breaking in to places, even if we can't get the goods on them. There hasn't been any of that talk. And when I called the water company people about the reservoir buyouts, they said Nettie had signed everything and hadn't made any more fuss than most the others who are losing their land. A lot less than Greaves."

"Someone from outside the county?"

Grace sniffed. "Accidently stumbling onto Nettie's trailer way out there and down in that holler? At night, you can't even see her house lights from the road."

"I hope to hell it isn't something like that. With no ID on that one set of prints and after this long, we'll never catch a drive-by killer."

"So we have to hope the motive's either her land, the trees, or those coins."

I nodded in the dark. "All three pretty solid motives."

We had turned south on OK 69 and were approaching Wagoner. Grace's phone blared with the Star Wars theme. She scooped it from the dash shelf, glanced at the number, and answered officially, "Chief Deputy Torres." She listened intently, then said, "We're twenty minutes out. Keep someone watching his room and on the exits. We'll meet you in front of the Casino. We'd like to assist with the takedown." The caller seemed to agree.

"They found him," she said when she disconnected. "He wasn't at the Best Value Inn. The night manager told the police he's been walking down to the Creek Nation Casino every evening for dinner and stays until about 1:00 a.m. The police are watching his room and have a plainclothes officer on him in the Casino. They'll have a couple of officers ready to go in with us when we get there."

"Perfect timing," I muttered. "Maybe we're about to find out if this is about land, trees, or Nettie's gold."

30

The plainclothes officer with the Muskogee PD had located Verl at a quarter slot machine near the center of the playing floor. I'd never given the old boy credit for being especially bright, but he'd picked an end-of-the-row machine that positioned him to bolt quickly in any direction.

Three officers waited beneath the MUSKOGEE in yard-high block letters that spanned the Casino's main entrance. I introduced myself and Grace to the three, directing most of my attention to the blue-uniformed officer, a Lieutenant Jacobson. He deferred to one of the men in khaki pants and black shirts with a round patch over the left pocket that read "Muskogee (Creek) Nation Lighthorsemen." His name tag said "Sergeant Denson."

"Sorry Sergeant. I wasn't familiar with the protocols."

He waved off my concern. "The tribal police have jurisdiction on casino property. I'll be coordinating this arrest. What's your man wanted for?"

"Assault with a deadly weapon on a state patrol officer. He's also a suspect in another murder case."

The men's faces sobered and the Lighthorseman with Denson shuffled nervously, staring into the concrete walk.

"Did the officer survive?" Denson asked.

"He missed her. By sheer luck she was ducking out of the way."

"Should we expect him to be armed?"

"What are the conceal and carry laws here?"

"We're a concealed carry state, just like Missouri, but not in the casino. The law restricts weapons from places that offer pari-mutuel wagering."

I glanced toward the wide glass doors that opened into the casino. "The law won't be a deterrent. It'll be more a matter of whether he thinks someone's looking for him, how much he wants to resist, and whether he could get a weapon. He usually has a rifle with him. What does your man inside think?"

"Your guy has on a jacket."

"Then we need to approach him as if he's armed and will resist."

Denson glanced at the weapons Grace and I had strapped to our hips. "You two aren't law enforcement here so better not be carrying those inside. I suggest you take this door and your deputy the fire exit around the side. We'll try to collar him without a fuss and bring him out. If he gets away from us for some reason, don't shoot the sonofabitch. But you can try to detain him till we can give you some help."

Grace didn't like the instruction. "If he comes my way, can I draw on him?"

"I'm just saying 'don't shoot,'" Denson repeated. "For your sake. You're just regular citizens here and this is Creek Nation land."

"Another plan," I suggested. "How about Grace and I go in there unarmed, tell Verl your people are at every door, and invite him to follow us peacefully out of the Casino. Then there won't be cops walking through the place making people nervous. If he runs, you can stop him when he comes out."

Denson shook his head, frowning grimly. "If he's armed, he'll be likely to pull a gun in there if he thinks you're not."

I persisted. "Stand where he can see you from where he is. I don't think he'll pull a gun if he can see armed officers."

"If I were in his shoes, I'd grab a hostage or two and force my way out," Denson argued. "You two stay outside and let us do our job."

I shrugged. "Fine by me. If he runs, are you going to try to get a shot off in there? I don't think so. But we'll be ready out here."

Grace headed around the building toward the side exit, and I followed the three officers to the entrance to the playing floor. The plainclothes officer stood beside a row of slots near the center of the noisy room, watching for his men to enter. He turned and nodded behind him at a man who sat with his back to us, mechanically pushing a button on a brightly lit digital machine.

The officers spread out, Denson waiting until one of his tribal police had circled Verl's position and appeared in a back aisle. Lieutenant Jacobson was on the left flank, and the plainclothes detective had eased off to the right. Denson released the snap on his holster, walked briskly to a position beside Verl's right shoulder, and said something only the suspect could hear. Verl stopped manipulating the machine, lifted his hands away from his hips, and stood slowly, turning toward Denson. The three other officers closed from each side.

Verl's hands suddenly shot forward into Denson's chest, sending him sprawling backward into the path of the plainclothes officer. Greaves sprinted for the main door, throwing aside a waitress and sending her tray of drinks crashing to the floor behind him.

The entrance in which I stood was wide enough for him to dodge around me in either direction, calling for an open field tackle on a bull of a man running with a full head of steam. With him still looking back to determine the degree of his pursuit, I stepped quickly onto the Casino floor and bent forward into the face of the nearest gaming machine. As he reached the row, I swung a forearm out across his craning neck, clotheslining him just below the chin. His head shot up and knees buckled as he seemed to stretch out in mid-air for a fleeting second, then flopped onto his back with a breath-crushing thud.

Denson and the plainclothes officer were on him in an instant, weapons drawn as they probed his sides for a firearm. Verl lay gasping for breath, eyes bulging and lips turning crimson.

"Better check him for a crushed throat," I said, rubbing at my bruised wrist.

Verl coughed and spat a stream of red phlegm onto the carpet beside his face. He shook himself and pushed onto his elbows, glaring up at me with dark, angry eyes.

"I almost bit my tongue off, Tate," he gurgled, spitting another stream of blood onto the floor.

"Shouldn't have tried to run," I said, grabbing his jacket shoulder and pulling him upward. Denson caught a wrist and snapped on a cuff, pulling the arm backward and securing the other hand.

"We'll take him to the station up on Third," Denson growled, shoving Verl toward the outer door. "You can work with the local PD on what you want to do with him. Aside from resisting arrest, he hasn't broken any tribal laws. I'd just as soon not have to mess with him."

Lieutenant Jacobson took Verl by the bicep. "I've got him. I appreciate you men coming down to assist." He turned to me. "You can question him at the station. If we need to, we'll hold him while you work on extradition. Just follow me."

The interrogation room in the Muskogee station looked just like a CSI set: bare walls except for the cameras, an empty metal table, and three chairs: one on the suspect's side and two for interrogators. A one-way mirror filled half of one wall, not intended to fool the perp, but letting him know he was probably being watched by more than the people in the room.

Grace and I sat across from Verl who had been right about his tongue. We had waited almost two hours while an emergency room doctor at St. Francis Hospital stitched up the gash his teeth had created as I'd jolted his head back. It was now a few minutes before 2:00 a.m. Verl's jaw rolled uncomfortably as he flitted the sutured tongue around the inside of his mouth.

"I can't talk good with this, so you may as well let me go," he mumbled like a kid with a mouthful of dry popcorn.

"If we don't talk to you tonight, you're staying right down the hall," I promised. "If you have the right things to say, you can walk out of here tonight."

"You got no reason to hold me. You had to let me go back in Missouri."

"That was before LJ and Galen Suskey told us you had been over to Nettie's house to tell her you were cutting her trees."

Verl's jaw quit moving and his eyes half disappeared into a deep frown. "What the hell you talkin' about?"

"We had a long talk with Nettie's brother. He told us LJ was the one who's been feeding him information about what was happening with the water buyout. According to him, LJ told him on the phone that Nettie was dead and that you'd been over to let her know Galen was letting you cut trees. So we went up to the hospital and had a visit with LJ. He said the same thing."

Verl had to think about that for a few awkward moments. Then he said, "Then they must have told you I found the old lady dead."

"Yes, they did. But they also said no one went back over there to check on your story that she'd been dead awhile."

Verl shook his head firmly. "I told Pa he wouldn't want to be going on over there."

"And why was that, Verl? So no one would know you'd just killed her?"

The head shake became an exaggerated wag. "Hell, no. You could almost smell the death from our place. I knew when I got close that the old lady had died. And from more than the stink. That half-dead oak beside her trailer was crawlin' with buzzards. Maybe twenty of 'em. All eyeing her place like it was fresh roadkill."

I'd seen the buzzard tree. If Verl had killed the old woman, I doubted he'd have gone back again after the vultures had gathered.

"If you're telling the truth, Verl, why did you try to run tonight?" Grace asked.

He sneered around his swollen tongue. "Why'd I run? I looked up and cops was closin' in on me from all sides. I'd just been let out of jail by *you*, and I figured you'd come up with some other reason to give me grief."

"Like that you'd taken a shot at a state patrol officer?"

Verl's head shake stopped abruptly and he glared hard at me. "Damn it, Tate. You're trying to set me up for somethin', no matter what. I shot that tree to warn you off. Didn't even know there was no one with you."

"Not that shot, Verl. Just after Officer Torres here let you out of jail, you fired on the state patrol officer who was helping me with the Suskey case."

"That woman who shot LJ? The hell I did! Where did this happen?"

"We were checking on some evidence along the creek behind Nettie's house. You fired down from the ridge road. We found the casing from your Marlin in the brush up there."

Verl stopped rocking. "T'weren't from my gun. Hell, the minute I got out of that cell, I hightailed it out to the house and left the gun, then came here. That Marlin's in the house with my other guns. I 'spect you went back and searched the place. You must have found it."

"We did search, and the Marlin wasn't there."

Verl's troubled frown creased more deeply. As he thought, his eyes flitted nervously beneath heavy brows, then widened suddenly, staring into the tabletop. "That little shit," he mumbled around his thick tongue.

"Who we talking about here, Verl?"

He continued to glare at the table, his jaw again twitching into motion. After a moment he looked across at me and mumbled "Galen Suskey,"

I looked at Grace who asked what I was thinking. "Why are you thinking Galen Suskey, Verl?"

"He called me when I was about halfway over here. He'd just come into town and was at the house, wonderin' where me and Pa was hangin' out. I told him about you comin' down to the house and Pa getting shot and me spendin' the night in jail. He must have took the Marlin."

"How did he get to it without getting shot by one of your booby traps?" I wondered aloud.

Verl shook his head dismissively. "He knew about them. Knew where we set them up and how to unhook the wires. And you could get to the guns without goin' near one of them. They was right there by the back door."

"But why would he shoot at Tate and the state officer?" Grace asked. "He thought he might be getting the land and didn't seem too concerned about giving you permission to cut timber."

Verl sneered as much as his tender mouth allowed. "There was somethin' else Nettie had he thought he could get. Never would say what it was, but talked like some day when he got the place, it would make him rich. He must of thought you was lookin' for it."

I sat back and watched Verl massage the tongue for a few moments. If he'd been a village elder in Anbar Province, I'd have judged him to be telling me the truth. "Give us a minute," I said and nodded for Grace to follow me out of the room.

Lieutenant Jacobson was watching from the observation room. I directed my question to both of them.

"What's your gut telling you about what he's said?"

Jacobson glanced back through the window at the man who now hunched defiantly over the table, staring at the mirrored wall in front of him.

"Whether he's telling the truth or not may not be your challenge," the lieutenant said. "If two people say he came back from the victim's house and said she was dead, and if the time he says he went over there follows your time of death by much, that's going to be hard to pin on him. Same with the shot from the road. We can probably get a check-in time at the motel here and see what time it took him to get here after you released him. I assume you have a pretty accurate time on when the shot was taken."

I nodded. "That would be a great help. Can you call the motel?"

He chuckled. "I'd better send someone. They aren't likely to give out that kind of information over the phone." He disappeared back toward the front of the building.

"And you, Grace. How did he strike you?"

Her mouth flattened into a tight line. "It's hard for me to make an unbiased judgment. The guy's such a troublemaker, I don't like to give him the benefit of the doubt on anything. But Jacobson here has a point. We really don't even have any circumstantial evidence but the casing. And we haven't been able to match it to Verl's Marlin. I don't think we've got enough to ask for extradition, or even to hold him."

Officer Jacobson joined us again in the observation room. "I was wrong," he grinned. "I called Best Value Inn to tell them I was sending someone over, and they just gave me the check-in time. 11:15 a.m."

"About two hours after we were shot at," I muttered. "He couldn't have made it here by 11:15." The two looked at me questioningly as I thought out loud. "So maybe it *was* Galen who took the shot. Verl seems to think he knew there was value in the family property that we might discover. And Verl loaded the gun, which would explain the prints."

"But the union people and his old workmate put Galen in Bartlesville the day before and after the murder," Grace reminded me.

"Yes, they did," I agreed. "And I doubt the union people were lying." I worked my way mentally across the case board we had set up on the wall of my office. We had a set of prints from the crime scene that didn't match anyone on the wall and no one in the federal or state print banks. But I felt certain it belonged to someone connected to one of those photos. Who was linked, but hadn't been printed? Angela Pogue? She seemed too genuinely shaken by word of Nettie's death to be faking her grief, but stranger things had happened. Galen's buddy Calvin up in Bartlesville? Miguel in the back room of old Mr. Pogue's little shop in Mazatlán? If I'd only had the sense to try to get prints on each of these unlikelies, or picked up something they'd . . . .

It struck me like the proverbial bolt out of the blue. I pulled my wallet from my hip pocket and carefully extracted an embossed card from Mazatlán Numismatics, the one the silent Miguel had handed me from Pogue's desk.

"Lieutenant," I said, holding up the card by its corner, "I could use a small evidence bag for this. And could you print off a copy of the mugshot we sent over on Verl? I'll give you a site where you can also get one of his father, LJ Greaves. If you would, please, keep the copies print-free. We'll swing by for them in the morning. And I think we can let our prisoner go."

Jacobson looked skeptical. "You don't want to hold him for resisting arrest?"

"I don't. You can if you wish. But he'll be nothing but a pain in the ass. If this goes the way I think it will, we won't be trying to extradite him." Jacobson left and, a moment later, appeared on the other side of the mirror window, motioning for Verl to leave.

I pulled out my cell and dialed the office number, waited for Marti's voicemail to activate, and recorded a message.

"Marti, there's an invitation on the top right-hand corner of my desk. To a CASA appreciation dinner in Springdale, Arkansas. Have Rocky take prints from it and send them up to

Officer Joseph. Some will be mine. It's the others I'm interested in. Thanks. See you tomorrow afternoon."

"Afternoon?" Grace asked.

"Yup. Let's go get a few hours sleep. Tomorrow morning we're headed up to Bartlesville."

31

The fourplex on South Creek Avenue in Bartlesville was a red brick box of a place that looked exactly like three others strung end-to-end along the east side of the street. Each had a walk-through passage between apartments on both floors, leading to rear balconies on the upper level and patios below. Apartment A was on the bottom left. We circled the block and could see a gas grill and two plastic lawn chairs sitting on the concrete apron behind the Latty unit. Curtains drawn. No sign of anyone home. But a white Honda Civic pulled into a short drive that connected to an alley between streets.

Before turning in the night before, we'd held a quick strategy meeting.

"You've been waiting for a chance to wear civvies on the job," I grinned at Grace. "Tomorrow's your day. Did you bring any with you?"

"I brought jeans to wear home," she admitted. "I like to be in uniform, but thought we were just driving home."

"Just uniform shirts?"

She reddened slightly. "No. A T-shirt too."

"Anything written on it?"

"It's a Chiefs T-shirt. I'm tired of seeing St. Louis getting all the attention in the office."

"I'd hardly say one morning with Joseph in a Blues shirt is lots of attention."

"A *wet* Blues shirt. And you're always wearing that Cardinals shirt."

"Only wet because we'd just climbed out of the creek."

"Yes. And she still had hers on." Grace grinned as if this was all just being playful, but the undertone of resentment seeped through.

"Well, wear the jeans and T-shirt tomorrow. I'll be dressed the same. This guy hasn't seen either of us. I don't want him thinking 'cops' if he looks through the curtains."

"It's supposed to be cold in the morning. Maybe rainy."

"All the better. We'll swing by Wal-Mart, get a couple of light jackets and some gloves."

"I don't think it's going to be 'gloves' cold."

"If it's even chilly, he won't notice. And I want gloves when we go to the door."

We had been sitting across a table in the breakfast area at the Holiday Inn Express, watched by a curious night clerk who wondered what we had to talk about at 3:00 a.m. Grace had mixed a cup of hot chocolate and took a sip, watching me over the top of the jacketed paper cup. "I should go to the door by myself," she said cautiously.

"No way. We go up together."

"Why is it," Grace said indignantly, "that you can go out on potentially dangerous calls all the time without backup, but you always make sure someone's with me? I'm almost safer if Frankie doesn't go. And he goes by himself. Rocky does. But never me. Did you allow your little partner from the state to go up to the Greaves by herself?"

I leaned back in the molded plastic chair. "No. I didn't. In fact, she'd disappeared into the woods when I confronted the Greaves. Came up behind them."

"But you wouldn't have. You don't think we can handle these things alone."

"That's not it at all. I just don't want to put you in harm's way without backup."

"Because you think you did that once."

"That's got nothing to do with this."

"It has everything to do with tomorrow. It makes the most sense for me to go to the door alone. A young woman, looking a little confused like she can't find the right apartment? He'll open for me when he won't for a couple. You cover the back."

"We'll figure that out when we get there," I begged off. "Better get some sleep."

The weather and the layout of the apartments made the decision simple. A cold front out of West Texas was making its way up I-44, bringing with it low, moody clouds and occasional drizzle. Jackets and light gloves made sense. The passage between apartments allowed me to stand in the cut-through, close enough to hear what was going on and get around to the front if Latty gave Grace trouble. It also put me in good position to run for the back if he bolted out a rear door.

We parked a block away. The rain was giving us a break. I slipped across the front of Apartment B and into the breezeway while Grace decided to play her role to the hilt. She walked up and down the street sidewalk, holding one of the mug sheets we'd been given as if it were a street guide and checking apartment numbers in apparent confusion. She finally shrugged in frustration and walked resolutely up to the first apartment in the set, rapping sharply on the door. It opened quickly enough that I knew Grace had been right. The occupant had been watching the pretty brunette in the snug jeans through the window, wondering if he should step out and offer assistance.

"Can I help you?" The voice was a raspy male.

Grace continued the role as we'd planned it during the drive. "Yes. I think you can." She separated a second sheet she held behind the first photo and handed both to the man, forcing him to take one in each hand.

"I'm Officer Grace Torres from Crayton, Missouri. I assume you're Calvin Latty. We spoke a few days ago on the phone about Galen Suskey's stay with you. I wondered if you could give me a little more assistance?"

There was a pause, then the man said, "What's that you got on you there? That a bodycam?"

I knew Grace was looking down with visible surprise at the small, black box she had clipped to her jacket pocket. "Oh, yes. That's routine now. Mainly for your benefit. I forget it's there."

"So, you're filming me? What do you want? I told you what I know."

"Just a couple of questions. I don't need to come in. We can talk right here. Did Galen have any visitors while he was staying with you? Either of these men?"

Grace had handed the photos to the man upside down, and there was a moment of muffled shuffling as he turned the two mugshots in his hands. "No. Never seen either of these guys. And no one come to see Galen while he was here."

"Thank you," Grace said gratefully, taking the sheets and folding them together, tucking them back into an inner jacket pocket."

"Did he talk regularly on the phone with anyone while he was here?"

"He'd call some people. But not a lot. And I don't know who, for sure."

"You didn't know who any of them were?"

"Well, some, I guess. He called the union office at least every day. The company had messed up his pension somehow and they were helping him. I heard him talk to them. I don't know who else."

"Did he ever mention a sister?"

"You asked me that when you called before. Like I said then, he didn't say nothing about a sister."

"Oh, yes. I forgot I asked. But as I remember, you told me he left here to take care of some family business back home in Missouri. He didn't say what it was?"

"Something about an old family farm. Somebody told him they was going to flood it for a water deal of some kind."

"And what did he think he was going to do about it?"

"No idea. He just felt like he needed to go over there."

"Well, thank you," Grace said graciously. "I think you've told me what I needed to know."

"You come all the way over here for that?"

"For the pictures," she said, patting her pocket. "I needed to show you the pictures."

"Who are they?" It struck me as a bit unusual that Latty hadn't asked when she first showed them.

"A couple of people of interest in a case we're investigating," Grace said.

"Oh, yeah? What kind of case?"

Grace had started to turn from the door, but swung back to answer. "Galen had a sister who was still living on the family farm. Somebody killed the woman."

"You're shitting me! When did this happen?"

"A couple of days before Galen came back to town. That's why I was curious about calls. It's kind of surprising no one called him about it."

"I don't think Galen talked to anyone over there. He'd been gone a long time."

Grace gave that a moment's thought. "Someone told him about the farm being flooded."

"Yeah. But that was a while back."

"And whoever that was didn't think it would be just as important to let him know his sister had been killed?"

I could hear Latty shuffle nervously in the doorway. "Like I said, he talked to people sometimes, but he never said nothing about a sister—or her being killed."

"Hmm," Grace murmured. "Well, I think that's everything. Thank you, Mr. Latty. I'll give you a call if I think of anything else you might be able to help us with. You going to be around town?"

"Yeah. I ain't going nowhere."

Grace turned down the walk until the door closed behind her, then took a sharp left back toward the parked car. I slipped through the breezeway and cut down the alley behind the fourplexes, beating her to the Explorer.

"Very nicely done," I said as she approached.

She grinned broadly. "And without backup. Interesting looking guy. Not what I expected." She unclipped the bodycam. "I'll plug it into the computer while we drive."

"The station's only ten blocks away. Let's drop these prints off with the card I picked up in Mexico, get them made up and sent to Officer Joseph, and head home. I'm sure you don't want to spend another night on the road."

"It's actually been kind of nice," she said.

32

The rain followed us up I-44, slowing traffic on the Will Rogers Turnpike to what still seemed to me racetrack speeds for wet pavement. One of the great lessons of law enforcement is that going 80 miles an hour is dangerous under the best of conditions. When the road surface is wet and when semis are throwing up spray, the slightest mishap can send a car spinning sideways out of control. And I'd say maybe one percent of drivers know how to steer out of a skid. The other ninety-nine, when going too fast, are accidents waiting to happen.

Grace played the bodycam video as we drove, showing the man standing in the doorway of Apartment A. He was almost twice Galen Suskey's size, a typical roughneck who had once been tough as the job he did, but had now begun to go to seed. Belly sagging. Shoulders beginning to stoop. Arms still thick, but showing some looseness in the leathery skin.

"You said, 'Not what I expected,'" I said to Grace. "What were you expecting?"

She flashed an embarrassed grin. "There was something else I didn't mention about our man Galen when I checked up on him. I learned that he's had a few male friends in for the evening while he's been staying at the Super 8. Some you'd know from around town."

I guessed from her tone that she wasn't talking about some of his old contacts. "Some evening entertainment?"

"Exactly. And I guess it shows some stereotyping on my part, but Calvin didn't look like I'd imagined."

My thought jumped to the two teenaged boys who had been each other's only friends in Blackjack Holler years ago: one who felt like he needed to get out of town as soon as he could break away, and the other who'd turned into a bitter, mean old recluse. Grace again seemed to read my thoughts.

"You're thinking LJ, aren't you?" she guessed.

I didn't answer. Just kept thinking.

We left the interstate at Afton and headed due east on Highway 60 into Missouri, passing another three or four casinos before we crossed the state line. Grace suddenly seemed more interested in talking local school politics than reviewing the case, leaving me with the feeling that as we neared home, she wanted this to feel more like a couple of friends out for a cross-country drive than like two colleagues gathering evidence.

"So, what do you think about this new four-day school week proposal?" she asked.

I'd been mentally calculating odds of one of our three print possibilities coming up positive. It took a minute to recalibrate.

"I don't like it," I offered finally. "Dumb idea."

"Why? The argument is that it reduces bussing and utility costs and gives teachers an extra prep day to take an in-depth look at individual student needs and performance."

"You sound like the little video they're running on their Facebook page."

"Well, those are the arguments."

I shrugged, finding I was also enjoying talking about something other than business. "I don't have a dog in this fight—or a kid, I should say—so I probably shouldn't be vocal about it. But it all seems bass-ackward to me in all kinds of ways."

"Yeah? Like what? My youngest sister and brother are still in school. They think it would be great. Fridays off to get an extra day they can work."

As we'd separated ourselves from the interstate, the weather seemed to have decided to stay with the faster traffic. The overcast was breaking above us and, ahead, we could see patches of blue sky.

"Looks like things may be clearing up," I said, leaning forward over the wheel to peer upward.

"Don't change the subject," Grace complained. "I really want to know what you think about this."

I leaned back and cast her an amused glance. "Why? Like I said, I've got no kids and don't plan on any for a while. This isn't going to affect me."

"Now, you're starting to sound like the voters you complain

about all the time. What happened to 'What's good for the community is good for all of us?' And you're never planning to get married?"

"I thought we were talking about a four-day school week."

"*You* brought up having kids."

"No. I brought up *not* having kids. And you're right. I do care about the school decision because of what I think it means for the community." It was time to get things back on track. "I don't think it's a good idea."

"Well, I'm asking because you're one of the more thoughtful people I know. You've been lots of places and have pretty well thought-out ideas. What don't you like about it?"

"What are the major complaints you hear about schools right now?" I asked, hoping I could get her to answer her own question.

She frowned thoughtfully. "That they aren't preparing kids to be good workers."

"Or. . . ?"

"That they aren't getting kids ready for college."

"Or. . . ?"

"That kids aren't prepared to deal with all the stuff they have to face when they step into the real world. Family. Finances. Civic responsibility. That sort of thing."

"Okay. So we're falling short in three pretty critical areas of life preparation. Does that suggest we should spend *less* time at it? We already have kids in school for fewer days and hours than any country except maybe Uganda. So we want to give them even less preparation to compete with those other kids in the work world than we're giving them now?"

Grace laughed in a way that made her eyes shine and her face even prettier. "And you say you don't have a dog in this fight? That's quite a thought-out speech for someone who doesn't care about the decision."

"I didn't say I didn't care. Just that I wasn't sure I should be influencing others' decisions about it."

"Well, you're influencing mine, and that's why I asked. Are you going to. . . ."

Before she could put me on the spot again, my cell rang. I had it slaved to the Bluetooth in the Explorer and the number showed as Marti's. I poked the answer button.

"Hey, Marti. Do you have some news for us?"

Marti chuckled through the phone. "Some good news and some not-so-good news."

"We're on the road, as you can probably hear, and you're on speaker. We're probably an hour away. Give us a little good news."

"Officer Joseph called from Springfield. They've matched the three print sets you sent in with our mystery prints and had a positive."

I slapped the wheel and would have whooped out loud if Grace hadn't been with me. She wasn't as restrained and let out a gleeful "All right!"

"So, who was it?" we asked in unison.

"Well, that's where the not-so-good news comes in. She wouldn't tell me. She's headed down here and said she wants to tell you in person."

My mind raced through the possibilities. Why wouldn't Joseph just say who it was? Or call on my phone and tell me while I was on the road? Looking over at Grace, I could see the same thoughts running through her head.

"How long ago did she call, Marti? When do you expect her to get there?"

"She just called. But it sounded to me like she was calling from her car. It could be any time."

"Well, if she beats us there, tell her we're right behind her."

"I'm sure she won't say anything until you get here. She was pretty tight-lipped."

I glanced at the GPS. "Forty-eight minutes, Marti. That's when we'll be there."

"Okay. See you both then."

I touched the red disconnect button and looked over at Grace who had shifted beneath her seatbelt to partially face me. "What do you make of that?" she asked before the call disappeared from the dash display.

"She may just be being cautious. Knows how fast word moves around town, even when you think there's complete secrecy."

"Surely she would trust Marti. No one is more careful than

Marti."

"She wouldn't know that."

Grace shook her head. "I think it's because it's the girl. The Pogue daughter. I could tell from what she said about that visit that she really liked the girl. She wants to think this all through herself before you talk."

"Nah. It's the Mexican enforcer. That man, Miguel. She realizes he's essentially out of reach and wants to talk about next steps. We'd never get anyone extradited from Sinaloa State if we could even locate the guy again. And if it's his print, it means old Rufus Pogue was involved. My guess is it will be just as difficult to get him back in the country."

"That would also mean the Springdale people may be tied up in this somehow," Grace ventured.

"Hmm. Not necessarily. I can see old Rufus sending his man up to see if he could locate the coins without his son knowing about it." We rode for a few miles in silence, wondering if the old man would have Nettie killed without involving the rest of his family.

"Then again," Grace said, "it might be Calvin Latty. Officer Joseph would definitely want to keep that secret until you talked. Nettie's brother would be complicit and would be gone in a flash if he got wind we were on to him. And with Galen talking to LJ every day, the Greaves might have had a hand in it with them."

I couldn't stifle a laugh. "What we're saying is, we're pretty sure it isn't Brenda. Aside from that, we have no idea."

She smiled grimly, straightening in the seat. "Unless Brenda knew she was about to be cut out of Nettie's will and made some kind of a devil's bargain with Nettie's brother—or the Greaves."

"Okay," I conceded, the laugh fading. "I guess Brenda's back in."

33

Much to Marti's relief, we beat Joseph to the office.

"The woman is so . . . so 'official' about everything," she complained. "I don't know what I would have done with her if she'd come in before you got here."

"Made her sit and wait," I chuckled.

Marti sniffed. "She's not the 'sit and wait' type. And if she knows something important to this case, why couldn't she trust me to pass it along to you? Does she think I just sit here on my phone and gossip with people around town about what we're doing?"

Joseph *had* shown a basic mistrust for our office security. But I'd assured her she didn't need to worry about Marti. Rocky was our gossip. He swore it wasn't true, but when I needed to leak something into the community, a casual sharing with Rocky did the job. After one such breach, Grace had encouraged me to fire the man. But I'd pointed out that there were times when we wanted company secrets to get out, and every office needed someone you could count on to be a reliable "you didn't hear this from me" kind of source. Rocky was ours. When we truly needed to keep something confidential, it never made it to Rocky's ears.

"I'd decided if she got here before you did, I would send her over to the courthouse to pick up a record," Marti said. "Judge Werner's office called. Able's legal aide found a file copy of an old will from Nettie's parents and took it over to the courthouse. It left the farm to her."

"Who knows about it?" I asked. Able's office would be tight-lipped. But if Marjorie, the court secretary, had called it over, the word might be out. She was just what Joseph worried about.

"The judge called himself. He knows his office. But I don't know who else knows."

"Would you run over and get a copy? I need to get this

report filed."

I'd barely had time to open the screen on my desktop and Marti to grab her jacket when Joseph swept into the outer office, gave Marti a quick nod that didn't look distrustful, and pushed through my door with a perfunctory knock. She closed it behind her, but chose to remain standing by the door. Marti stayed where she was beside the coatrack, watching us through the glass.

Joseph leaned against the frame. "You got my message?"

I refused to look anxious and sat back casually in the chair. "I was told you had a positive on our mystery print but didn't feel that you could share it over the phone."

She grinned broadly. "I was just being dramatic. And selfish. I didn't want you moving on this without me being here to be part of it."

"Are we headed to Springdale?"

She looked momentarily confused, then shook her head dismissively. "No. Not the Pogues. And not your friend Miguel. The prints belonged to Calvin Latty. You sent us a very clear and complete set."

I reached for the phone.

"I've already called the Bartlesville police. They picked him up about an hour ago. That's why I'm a little late getting here. They wanted to know what we want done with him."

I got up from the desk and walked back into the outer office. "Grace, you want to come in here and be part of this?" She was sitting tight-jawed at her desk, but quickly grabbed a pad and followed me back into my sanctuary. I didn't look at Joseph to see if she approved. Grace took the chair by the window.

"Calvin Latty," I announced as she sat. "Calvin was in Nettie's trailer." Grace just lifted a brow as though she'd expected it all along. I waved for Joseph to take the other chair. "So we need to go pick up Galen. He had to either be with Calvin or be a willing accessory."

Joseph nodded. "Another reason I'm late. You'd given me Calvin's phone number earlier and I got one of our officers to check with his carrier about outgoing calls. He called Galen Suskey within minutes of the time you left his apartment. They talked for almost twenty minutes. But even if he's around, will he be at the motel at two in the afternoon?"

"Maybe not. But we'll know if he's still checked in. Have you got any better ideas about where to start looking?"

"Your case, Sheriff," she said, which meant "no."

I again rose from the desk. "I wonder if Latty called because he was suspicious or wanted to reassure Suskey we were following other leads? We'll probably find out when we get to the Super 8. If he's checked out, I'd guess he's running."

The desk clerk was the daughter of one of the Syrian families I helped with school conferences. A pretty girl named Raca who had adopted the dress of her new country so completely that, until she spoke, she could easily have been taken for any of the girls who grew up in Crayton. She had worked hard on losing her accent, but still spoke with the clipped English of someone who had grown up speaking Arabic. She told us Suskey was still checked in, but had walked past her half an hour earlier.

"Which direction?"

"Going out."

"Was he carrying his bags?"

"No. No bags.

"Can we take a quick look in his room?" I knew the girl was grateful for the help I gave her family and probably didn't know the first thing about warrants and room searches.

"Of course." She took a master key card from a drawer and led us down to 115. The room looked like the first Galen Suskey we had met: contained chaos with clothes and towels scattered across the floor and thrown loosely over a duffle that sat on the bag rack. Grace pulled on a pair of thin gloves and picked through the clutter while Joseph inspected the bathroom. I turned my attention to the closet. The sports jacket we had seen during his second visit to the office hung beside his one dress shirt.

"He wasn't dressed up when he left?" I asked Raca who watched curiously from the doorway.

"No, Sir. He was wearing very old clothes. And tennis shoes."

"Did you see which way he went when he left the lot?"

"I believe he was going into the town," she guessed.

"Did you see what he was driving?"

"A very old truck," she remembered. "It was red and gray."

I slid the closet door to the half-closed position I had found it in. "I think I may know where we can find him," I said. "Joseph, if you lose us, meet us at Nettie's place."

We parked at the top of the hill and walked as silently as the grassy verge allowed down to Nettie's trailer. The battered Ford F-150 stood in front, doors locked, but the passenger's window rolled down. I reached in, released the lock, and pulled the seat forward. A Marlin 336 lay on the floorboards below the rear window. Slipping on the gloves from my hip pocket, I lifted the weapon out and tossed it out of sight beneath the truck's bed, not certain who else might show up while we were down there.

Joseph knew where I was going and signaled that she would cut through the woods and circle the bend in the creek. I nodded and waved Grace to follow me.

Galen Suskey was so intent on keeping his footing on the mossy shelf and gripping the rock face that he didn't hear us step out onto the opposite bank just as Joseph appeared beyond the tangle of honeysuckle.

"You looking for something, Mr. Suskey?" I called loudly enough to freeze him against the bluff but not startle him backward into the pool.

He locked in place, knee-deep in the creek and clinging to a shallow recess in the ledge, his face pressed tightly against the cliff. His chest heaved a few times, then calmed.

"You're on my property," he called back. "And I'm just lookin' for what's mine, less'un you stole it from me."

"This isn't your property, Galen. The court found a copy of your parent's will. It left this all to Nettie. Did they call you about it?"

"They may have left the land to her, but that doesn't mean she got everything that might ha' been hid on it." The strain of gripping the rock and craning his neck showed in his voice.

"And what makes you think something might have been hid over there, Galen?"

209

"Maybe I talked to Nettie before she died. And maybe she told me something might be hid here."

"How long before she died, Galen? Just a few minutes? We just came back from talking to your friend Calvin. It seems he was over here talking to her also. What was that all about?" I thought fleetingly of letting him shuffle back off the ledge into shallow water, but decided the pressure of hanging on might loosen his tongue. He turned his face slowly across the rock slab in front of him, gazing downstream in Joseph's direction.

"Don't think about falling back into the pool," I warned. "It's over your head there and as you can see, the woman you shot at is waiting to haul you out down there."

He pressed his cheek more tightly against the cliff face and sputtered. "What the hell you talkin' about? I ain't shot at nobody. And Calvin don't even know about Nettie."

"Calvin's prints were in the house, Galen. He got picked up by the Bartlesville police after he called you this morning. That's not the story he's telling them. And when I match a casing we found up on the ridge road with that Marlin behind the seat in your truck, I think we might be able to make a case you tried to kill Officer Joseph. What kind of deal did you make with Calvin, Galen? Did you promise him half of the treasure you knew was hidden here somewhere?"

He trapped his eyes hard shut and locked his jaw. As I reached for the buckle of my gun belt, he threw himself backward into the pool, counting on my assurance that it was over his head. Before my weapon hit the ground, I was in the creek, splashing downstream into the pool.

I'd always thought that one of the worst possible ways of leaving this earth would be drowning, feeling that screaming in my lungs for air and the terror of knowing I couldn't hold out any longer. Galen Suskey didn't wait for that moment. In the clear pool, I could see him force out a breath and suck his lungs full of water. I dove forward, grabbed the man about his fleshy stomach and chest, and forced us both to the surface, squeezing as hard as I could. His head broke the surface and water sprayed like vomit from his lungs. I felt another pair of arms grab the man, and Grace struggled beside me as we waded and paddled to where Joseph reached from the bank for the limp figure.

We pushed him out of the creek as she dragged. I scrambled after him, straddling the still form and pushing hard again against the man's chest. I flipped to the side, making a quick swipe of his mouth to clear his tongue, then blew three breaths into his gaping mouth. Grace struggled to the other side and began to pump his chest. After the second sequence of breaths, he coughed up another stream of water and fought his way onto his side where he sputtered and shook the rest of the fluid from his lungs.

"You should have let me go," he gasped finally, glaring through red, swollen eyes.

I grabbed one shoulder and Joseph the other, hauling him to his feet.

"I need you to testify against Calvin," I said. "And for him to look you in the eye when he tells the court you talked him into killing your sister."

34

Galen had known the story of the Confederate treasure since he was a kid, but never believed it. Then, in a conspiratorial conversation with LJ Greaves about how he might be able to get part of the sale proceeds from the farm, his old pal mentioned that Nettie seemed to have found a way to live off practically nothing. Somehow, Greaves told him, the old woman had gained access to a sizable number of hundred dollar bills.

Calvin Latty, who had injured his back in the oil fields, initially found relief in opioids until his physician and insurance company cut off his supply. He quickly learned that street drugs were cheaper and easier to get, but still at a cost Calvin couldn't afford. When his old roustabout buddy, the only relationship the two were willing to admit to, promised him half a fortune if he would drive over into Missouri, smother an old woman who was probably close to death anyway, and see if he could find her source of income, Calvin's cravings answered for him. He'd killed Nettie Suskey with a plastic bag over her head, straddling her in her chair with his massive bulk so she couldn't get her arms up to tear the bag away. But then there had been no treasure and no sign of where it was.

Galen had been on his way to search the property when he saw us easing along the side of the pool. He watched until we began to struggle with the rock slab and couldn't imagine any reason to do that unless we knew where the treasure was hidden. His second trip to the creek had been prompted by a call from Judge Werner's office, notifying him that his parents had left their estate to Nettie. He saw one last chance to find the gold before he disappeared permanently.

The little man swore in court that the shot he had taken at Officer Joseph was just to scare us off before we discovered the gold before he could get to it.

"I wouldn't shoot nobody," he told a jury of twelve already skeptical citizens from across the county. "Especially no state trooper. And if I'd shot to kill her, I'd a hit her." A superimposed image of Officer Joseph standing on the rock shelf with the bullet crater visible through her transparent silhouette showed that he would have hit her squarely in the head had she not fallen.

Calvin Latty was found guilty of murder. Galen Suskey of attempted murder and as an accessory to murder. Both, I hear, are not faring well in the state penitentiary.

Brenda Castoe, it turns out, is as decent a human being as I'd first imagined. She inherited Nettie's estate, discovered that the old woman had been working through the Pogues to sell her dollars, and worked out the same arrangement to market what were left. They managed to keep the number of remaining coins out of the news, leaving Mazatlán Numismatics free to announce each year that perhaps the last of the 1861-D Indian Princess dollars had come to light and would be auctioned to the highest bidder. When Joseph told Brenda that it really was true that Nettie had given serious thought to leaving her money to the local CASA chapter, Brenda committed half of Ezra Suskey's booty to the advocacy group for foster kids. The other half she committed to seeing the world she had always dreamed about visiting.

Joseph's transfer to St. Louis didn't come through. She came down to Crayton for the Suskey trial at which Calvin appeared as a state's witness in exchange for life rather than the death sentence. She hung around the office the afternoon after the verdict, filling us in on her conversations with Brenda and seeing if we had any reason to prosecute the Greaves.

"Old Darnell was right," she laughed as I walked her to her car in the late afternoon. "Not a single spit of human kindness between the two of them."

"I'm afraid we got nothing on them this time," I confessed. "Galen took the Marlin from the house when both of them were gone. But I suspect there will be a next time. Do you want in?"

She smiled in such a way that I couldn't help but suggest

that she didn't need to drive home so late. "And I could whip up some of my special pasta in no time."

"I don't think so, Tate." The smile didn't leave her lips. "But I've been thinking I didn't see the best of Mazatlán during my two-day visit. I might take a week sometime in the next few months and really get to know the old city. Should I give you a call?"

I shrugged uncertainly. "With *molcajete* and *tres leche* cake?"

"Every meal, if you like," she promised.

OTHER BOOKS BY ALLEN KENT

Unit 1 International Thrillers

The Shield of Darius
The Weavers of Meanchey
The Wager
The Marburg Mutation
Straits of the Between
Ring of Thorns

The Whitlock Trilogy (historical fiction)

River of Light and Shadow
Wild Whistling Blackbirds
Suzanna's Song

The Colby Tate Mysteries

Murder One
Eye for an Eye

Mystery/Thrillers

Backwater
Guardians of the Second Son

ABOUT THE AUTHOR

Allen Kent is the "USA Today" and Amazon bestselling author of the popular Unit 1 thriller series, the Colby Tate Mystery Series, and the celebrated Whitlock Trilogy in historical fiction. His books, with summaries, can be found at his website, https://allenkentbooks.com.